Here We Go Round

Here We Go Round

ALICE McGILL

Illustrations by SHANE EVANS

Houghton Mifflin Company
Boston 2002

www.houghtonmifflinbooks.com

The text of this book is set in 15-point Dante.

Library of Congress Cataloging-in-Publication Data
McGill, Alice
Here we go round / by Alice McGill ; illustrated by Shane Evans.
p. cm.
Summary: In 1946, seven-year-old Roberta goes to her grandparents'
North Carolina farm during the last month of her mother's pregnancy.
ISBN 0-618-16064-7
1. African Americans—Juvenile fiction. [1. African Americans—Fiction.
2. Babies—Fiction. 3. Grandparents—Fiction.] I. Evans, Shane, ill. II. Title.
PZ7.MI67565 He 2002
[Fic]—dc21   2001039249

Manufactured in the United States of America
HAD 10 9 8 7 6 5 4 3 2 1

To Symone' Gaither, Mokeela Brown,
and Karah Anderson—excellent readers

chapter one

It was summertime, June 1946, in Washington, D.C. Robert Robinson gave his final word that Saturday morning after breakfast. "Roberta," he said, sitting at the table with his fingers locked together.

"But Daddy, I'm seven years old now. I know how to be quiet and help Mama." Roberta pounded her words as fast as a jackhammer. "Why do I have to go to the country?"

"We have talked about this time and again," her father said, keeping his voice low so her mother wouldn't hear. "The doctor said your mother must stay in bed for one month. So you *are* going to North Carolina to stay with Gramma Louise and Grampa Dave for just thirty days— *that's all.*"

"But Daddy, I thought of something else," Roberta disagreed.

"When you come back, a new baby sister or baby brother will be waiting for you," her daddy replied, as if he could hardly wait.

The new baby was all he talked about, lately. She caught her breath. "But Daddy—"

"What?" her father asked, clearing the table. "Your Aunt Emma will be here soon. Get up and empty the ice pan—iceman's coming today. We're on the list to have an electric refrigerator delivered before you get back too," he reminded himself. "You sure everything's packed?"

"But Daddy," Roberta tried again, dragging the pan of water from under the icebox. "Why don't we go to the country and bring Gramma Louise and Grampa Dave back to stay here with us? Then all of us can be with Mama." She loved her gramma and grampa. Grampa Dave made the prettiest dolls out of corn shucks.

"Because they have to work the farm, baby girl," her father said.

"Oh," Roberta responded, dumping the water in the sink. She liked for her father to call her "baby girl." But Roberta had never visited her grandparents during the summertime. This morning her mother had reminded her to help Gramma Louise feed the chickens and pull weeds out of the garden and things like that. Her mother had eaten her breakfast upstairs in the bedroom. She had to stay in a quiet place and rest, like the doctor said.

Just then Aunt Emma knocked at the back door and opened it with a key. "The key works," she said gleefully, holding on to a big covered basket and kneeing her suitcase ahead, saying good morning too many times and too loud. "Everybody ready to go?"

"Well, I'm going down the street to the filling station and get a tank of gas, Emma," her daddy answered, leaving the kitchen. "We'll be ready to go Down South soon as I get back." That's what her daddy called the country—Down South.

"All my things are packed, Aunt Emma," Roberta told her mother's oldest sister.

"Well, well," Aunt Emma said with a laugh. "I brought fried chicken, potato salad, and coconut cake for the trip. Just think. Soon, a new baby in the family." Aunt Emma sounded like she was bragging.

"I know," Roberta almost screamed. "That's why Daddy painted that old ugly room and bought that baby bed and baby clothes. And that's why Mama is so fat!"

Aunt Emma flopped down in the chair, laughing like she couldn't catch her breath.

"Shhh!" Roberta put her finger to her lips and pointed toward the stairway.

"Oh, don't worry 'bout laughing," Aunt Emma chuckled. "Laughing is good for you. And don't you worry 'bout your mama while you're down there in Scotland Neck, North Carolina. I'll be right here looking out for her, every day."

"I know," Roberta sighed.

"That's where your daddy was born and raised," Aunt Emma added.

"I know. I have to talk to Mama now." Roberta went up the steps on tiptoe so the stairs wouldn't creak.

"*There* she is!" her mother exclaimed as if the movie star Lena Horne had entered the room. Her puffed-up pillows were starchy white. "Ready for that good country air and fresh vegetables anytime you want them?"

"I think so," Roberta answered. She knew she couldn't jump on the high, soft bed like she used to.

"You write to me every week, Roberta," her mother said, smiling.

"I know about addresses." Roberta was bragging now. "Just like Gramma Louise wrote: 'Mrs. Helen Robinson, 1387 Park Road, NW, Washington, D.C.'"

"Don't forget—every week," her mother said again.

"I won't ever forget," Roberta said, shaking her head. She could see herself sitting at Gramma Louise's front room table with her pencil and paper.

"You'll help me with the baby when you come back, won't you?" her mother asked.

"I don't like babies."

"Why?"

"Just don't." Roberta pushed the frilly curtains back and

looked out the window. Some people wearing sunglasses were walking by.

"You're going to be a big sister," her mother said.

"I'm already big."

"Come here, Roberta."

Roberta ran and threw her arms around her mother's neck without saying a word. She was careful not to touch the big ball-like stomach. Then her father entered the room.

"Time to go, baby girl," he said. "Emma took your suitcases downstairs."

"Bye, Mama."

"Don't say bye, say, see ya later."

"See ya later," Roberta said with a short laugh. She left the room because she knew her daddy was about to kiss her mother. She hated when they got all mushy. "Ugh," she said, hoping they had heard her.

Roberta slouched at the curb and watched Aunt Emma place the basket of food on the passenger side of the front seat.

"Y'all will be there by four o'clock," Aunt Emma said as her brother-in-law joined them at the car.

"I'll be back here by four o'clock tomorrow too, Emma." Her father looked up at the front bedroom window. He slammed the trunk shut.

Roberta didn't want Aunt Emma to kiss her. But her aunt kissed her anyway—five times. Finally, Roberta scrunched down in the back seat of her father's brand-new sedan. She liked the sweet rubbery smell of it. This space was hers.

The car had hummed down the streets and was out on the open road a long time before she rose up to look out of the window.

"Daddy, what does MPH mean—on that sign?" she asked as all sorts of signs whizzed by.

"Miles per hour."

"So you can't drive but fifty miles an hour," Roberta said.

"You sound like your aunt Emma," her father chuckled. "Bossy."

Roberta laughed and leaned back on the seat. It was a good thing her favorite aunt could stay with her mother. I'm going to write Mama soon as I get there, she thought. A mellow breeze streamed from the windshield and floated overhead. Roberta pushed her thick braids back from her face.

"You still back there, Roberta?" her daddy asked after a while.

"You know I'm back here, Daddy," Roberta said, smiling drowsily. If her daddy said any more she didn't hear it because sleep wouldn't let her.

He drove on and on without her being aware of that either. But she woke up to the sound of music as soon as the car stopped. She looked out of the window. They had parked in front of Buddy's Bar-B-Que, according to the red and black lettering on the sign. That's where the music was coming from.

"Take our dinner over to one of those tables under the trees," her daddy said as he handed her their basket, pointing to where some people were eating. "I'm buying us a bottle of pop." He disappeared into the music.

Roberta started off, but blues-playing guitars made her pause to listen for a few seconds. She rocked on her toes to the beat until she noticed people smiling at her from the tables. A gramma-looking woman waved. Roberta waved back and sat down on a bench and dug her feet under the table.

Her daddy joined her, carrying two bottles. Aunt Emma's fried chicken and potatoes tasted so good. A bite of coconut cake and a swallow of fizzy pop made her smack her lips. At home she would have had hot cabbages or something.

"Got to get back on the road," her father said after they had finished eating. He lifted his feet over the wooden bench and walked toward the car, bobbing his head to the beat of the music as if he was getting ready to dance.

Roberta groaned to herself. She grabbed the basket and followed, hoping that no one was watching him.

"Daddy," Roberta said with a laugh after they had been on the road again for some time. "Real grown people not supposed to dance."

"Real grown people?"

"You know, grown people who have chil—I mean like mamas and daddies."

"Now, Roberta," her father said, shaking his head. "Your mama and I dance all the time when we go out. We like dancing."

"Do other people see you dancing?"

"Of course."

"Oh, Daddy," Roberta moaned. I bet they look so silly, she thought.

"After the baby gets here, we might get the chance to dance again."

They can't think about anything but that baby, Roberta fumed to herself. She wanted her mother right then. It wouldn't do any good to tell him that though. "I'll be glad when we get to Scotland Neck," she said tiredly. "How long do we have now?"

"We've gone way over halfway. Emporia, Virginia, is behind us, baby girl."

"Oh, yeah, I saw the signs." She remembered that Weldon, North Carolina, was not far away. "Daddy, do you think Mama will feel like writing a letter to me?"

"Of course," her father assured her. "Your mama loves to write. It won't hurt her one bit." Her father glanced at her in the rearview mirror.

"Well, I'm going to write her a letter, every week just like she asked," Roberta affirmed.

"How about me, baby girl?" Her father pretended to whine like his feelings were hurt.

"Well, I'll drop a line to you too, Daddy." Roberta was happy now.

"We're passing the Colonial Inn," her daddy said about thirty minutes later, nodding his head to the right.

"I know," Roberta said without looking. "The Peterson farm is next."

Pastures of cows and horses grazing behind fences lined the road. Houses were a long ways apart. Roberta was getting tired of sitting. "Hope I didn't forget anything," she said almost to herself.

"Fine time to think of that now," her father said over his shoulder. "You had plenty enough time to get your things straight."

"Mama said I didn't forget anything." She met her father's eyes in the rearview mirror.

"Uh-oh!" he said suddenly, cutting the wheel sharply to the left and spilling her onto the floor. "You hurt, baby girl?" He glanced over his shoulder. "I almost missed the turn."

"No, Daddy, I'm not hurt." She scooted back onto the soft seat. The car wheels went plumpa-lump-plump-lump on the dirt road that led to her grandparents' farm. They passed the mailboxes near the big pine tree.

"I remembered to pack my new skates too," Roberta said excitedly.

"Oh, yeah? Skates?"

"Yes. I can skate all by myself now."

"Look out the window. Tell me what you see."

Roberta rose up. "I see fields of something growing, trees, Miss Ginny's house, the plum tree—I can't see any plums. There's the top of Miss Mabel's house—that's where Lena Mae lives—and there's Mister Joe Baker's hog pen."

"See any sidewalks?"

"No," Roberta answered slowly.

"You need a hard surface for roller-skating, Roberta."

"I know," she said, finally getting his meaning. "There's Gramma Louise!" Roberta yelled, forgetting about the skates.

"Well, well!" Her gramma's excited voice rose above the car's motor.

The car eased around the chinaberry tree and the sweet bessie bushes, almost to the corner of the front porch.

chapter two

"Gramma Louise!" Roberta shouted through the car window. "Stop the car, Daddy!"

"I thought y'all would never get here." Her grandmother glowed as Roberta jumped out of the car and ran up the porch steps and into her arms. "I been sitting here looking up that road and looking up that road."

"It took a long time," Roberta said. Her gramma always smelled like cinnamon. Her arms were soft and plump. "We left Mama in the bed, like the doctor said."

"She'll be all right, too." Her gramma patted her back.

"I have brought Roberta to you." Her daddy bowed like he was on a stage, leaving the car parked under the shady pines. "Brown skin car service from door to door. Who could want for anything more?"

"Nobody in this world," Gramma Louise exclaimed, rushing to meet her son. She glad-slapped him on the jaw several times.

Roberta watched her Gramma Louise's stomach shake

up and down when she laughed, as if happiness was all she cared about. The three of them hugged again. Her gramma's stomach was big but not round and hard like her mother's.

"Your papa be back directly. Had to go uptown and do something to that old truck."

"I smell something cooking, Mama," her father said.

"Supper's fixed already." Gramma Louise pulled open the screen door. "Y'all come on in."

The house smelled like apple pie and chicken and dumplings. Roberta stepped inside. A big hallway covered with shiny linoleum split the house in half from the front door to the back door. The squares on the linoleum could outline a hopscotch game. Photographs of old people hung on the wall in brown oval frames. The front room was to her left. That's where her daddy would sleep that night.

"It's half past four. Y'all find the wash pan and soap and all in the kitchen," Gramma Louise urged.

"Just let me cool out in this nice breeze for a minute, Mama," her father said, smiling. He eased himself into the rocking chair and stretched his legs out like Grampa Dave.

Gramma Louise took a fresh apron from a hook on the door. "Go out to the backyard and see how many chickens I got now," she told Roberta.

She and Daddy are gonna talk about something, Roberta

thought. She pushed on the back screen door and jumped down the narrow steps. The yard had been swept clean and every sprig of grass had been shaved away with a sharp hoe. Chickens and baby chicks were pecking in the grass near the coop. She didn't feel like counting chickens. So she sat on the bottom step.

"Your wife's not the only woman this happen to, Robert," she heard her gramma say, fussing a little bit.

"What happen to?" Roberta jumped up and peeped through the screen.

Her daddy laughed.

"My gracious," her gramma said. "Little heads got big ears. Come in here and tie my sash."

Roberta ran down the hallway.

"No running in the house," her father corrected.

Roberta stopped at her gramma's turned back. "Sorry," she said. It took some doing, but she made a long, droopy bow with the apron sash. Her gramma looked back and smiled. "What did you and Daddy say about Mama?" Roberta asked.

"Nothing bad."

"That's right," her daddy said.

"Do you think Mama's stomach will get any bigger, Gramma Louise?" Roberta asked with her eyes closed.

"Oh, Lordy," her gramma said.

Her daddy coughed.

"Why do you want to know so much 'bout grown folks business?" her gramma asked.

"If her stomach gets any bigger, it might crack open—like an egg."

The back screen door slammed. Roberta looked around. "Where did Daddy go?"

"He went out." Gramma Louise said with a knowing smile. "Men don't like to talk about such things. Is that what's worrying you, child—your mama's stomach?" Her gramma sat down in the rocking chair.

"A little bit."

"Well, don't you worry 'cause your mama's doing fine."

"That's what all of them say," Roberta said. The rocking chair wobbled back and forth like it was waiting on her to say something else. But she couldn't talk about what was really worrying her. It was her secret.

"Yonder he comes." Her gramma pointed to the swirling dust that followed Grampa Dave's blue pickup truck.

Roberta dashed out of the front door. Her grampa stopped and opened the door as soon as he saw her running on the side of the road. She climbed onto the oily-smelling seat beside him.

"Looka here, looka here." He leaned over and patted her on the back. The truck sounded like it sneezed before it jerked and moved off. "How long y'all been here?" he asked over the noisy engine.

"We just got here," Roberta half-shouted. He wore a vest from a worn-out suit over his work shirt. Pieces of folded paper stuck out of the pockets. "Gramma fixed supper."

"Good, good!" He said everything two times, just like Gramma Louise.

After supper, Grampa Dave put her suitcases in the back bedroom. Then he went to sit on the porch with her daddy. Their voices rumbled down the hallway.

Roberta heaved herself onto the bed and looked around. A new globe shade covered the oil lamp on the bureau.

Gramma Louise came into the room to help hang her best clothes in the wardrobe. "What pretty little dresses," she commented, stroking the ruffled collars.

"Mama said I can't play outside with my best clothes on," Roberta chatted. "I brought old dresses for playing." She laid socks and play clothes in the bottom drawer.

"Lots of little girls round here for you to play with when they ain't helping out in the field and all."

"I know," Roberta chirped, even though she didn't want to think about playing right then. She had only spent one or two days at a time in the country during the wintertime. "I think I want to write a letter to Mama," Roberta said, looking at her gramma.

"You'll find paper and envelopes in the—"

"I remember," Roberta said, rushing to the front room. The lined paper was in the drawer. She decided to use a pencil instead of Gramma Louise's ink pen. Ink dripped. Fading sunlight splashed through the window over the table. She sat down. In a little while, three pieces of paper lay crumpled on the floor. The next two letters were unsatisfactory too. Finally, without too much erasing, all of the words were in place, but the sunlight had left the window. Roberta strained her eyes to read out loud:

> *Dear Mama,*
>
> *I am here. We had chickin and dumplins*
> *for super.*
>
> *I am fine. Gramma Louise and Grampa Dave*
> *are fine. You are fine too.*
>
> *I miss you. Daddy is talking to Grampa Dave.*
> *Write me when you get this letter. I love you.*
>
> *Your child,*
> *Roberta*

"That's good," she said to herself and folded the letter into the envelope. "I'll write the address tomorrow."

Gramma Louise entered the room and walked to the table. "I need to light this lamp so your daddy can see when he comes in here," she said quietly. "It's about my bedtime."

Roberta watched her gramma lift off the lampshade and strike a long match on the rough side of a red and white matchbox.

"Time for you to go beddie-bye too."

"Yes, Gramma Louise." Roberta headed for her room. Her daddy and Grampa Dave were still talking when she put on her nightgown and slipped into bed. The house was nice and cool now. Before long, her daddy crept in and patted her on the head. She heard him blow the lamplight out before he crept away.

"Goodnight, Daddy." Her voice caught him before he reached the door.

"Goodnight, baby girl."

The next morning, Roberta awakened to a strange noise outside her room. She jumped out of bed and peered into the hallway.

"What you doing up so early?" Grampa Dave said, standing over a big box. "All the chickens ain't up yet."

"I thought I heard Daddy leaving," Roberta said, stepping outside the door in her nightgown.

"You think he'd leave without tellin' you?" Grampa Dave asked like she should have known better than to think such a thing. "That was me pulling this box of beans, ears of corn, and salad greens for your daddy to carry back for him and your mama." Grampa Dave dragged the box onto the front porch.

"Here's your bathwater, child," Gramma Louise placed a bucket of warm water outside the kitchen doorway. "I put a cake of soap and towels in your room." Then she rushed back to the breakfast smells before Roberta could tell her that she felt like crying. Her daddy would be returning home today. The thought of the baby still made her mad.

She lifted the bucket across the hall. The wood stove sent whiffs of smoke over the yard from the chimney. It was time for her to get dressed. Country people didn't walk around in their bedclothes during the daytime.

"Time to get out of here," her father said after everybody had eaten a big breakfast. He pushed himself away from the table. "Helen will be expecting me by four o'clock today."

"You don't want her to be worrying." Gramma Louise's face was quiet.

"No indeedy," her grampa agreed. His face was serious too.

Roberta ran out of the kitchen to her bedroom and searched under the pillow.

"What's wrong?" her daddy yelled, following after her.

Roberta met him in the doorway and handed him the letter. "I want you to take this to Mama. I wrote it last night."

"You did?"

"Tell her I'm going to address the envelope when I write to her again next week, like I promised." Roberta felt less sad when she gave the letter to her daddy. It made her feel grown up, to be writing letters home.

"I will tell her." His voice broke as he said this.

She watched him put the letter in his shirt pocket. "Don't lose it."

"Roberta, I am proud of you," her daddy said in a clear voice.

"Thank you, Daddy," she said. She watched him load his suitcase and the box of vegetables in the trunk. Her grandparents stood with her at the car. She wanted her daddy to hug her last, and he did—for a long time. The three of them waved until the car turned onto the hard surface and out of their sight.

chapter three

"You notice anything new in your room, Roberta?" Grampa Dave asked right away, with sneaky eyes just like her daddy had when he was about to say something funny.

"No."

"Well I noticed something new," her gramma said with a smile.

Roberta cut down the hallway. She jumped into her room and took a quick look around. Her nightgown was on the back of the chair—nothing in the chair or on the bed. The bucket of used bathwater was near the bureau. Then she noticed a ticking sound coming from the bureau.

"My own clock!" she squealed. Right beside the ivory colored clock was what looked like a gingerbread house, real enough to eat. It was about a foot high with two open front doors. A little old man with an umbrella was inside, and a little girl with a basket of flowers was on the outside.

"Notice anything new yet?" her grampa peeped around the door.

"Oh, thank you, Grampa Dave." Roberta rushed to him with clock in hand. "But what is that pretty little house for?"

"That's a weather house." He walked to the bureau. "See, the little girl's on the outside. That means it's gonna be sunshine. If that little old man comes out—"

"It's going to rain, because he has his umbrella." Roberta finished his sentence.

"That's right," her gramma said, admiring the new things from the doorway.

"Daddy sets his clock every night," Roberta chuckled. "Before I go to bed tonight, can you show me how to make the alarm go off, Gramma Louise?"

"Indeed so," her gramma said. "Then you can get out of bed when you want to—you'll know what the weather's gonna be too."

"Does it really tell the truth?" Roberta asked, rubbing the smooth roof lightly.

"We'll have to see," her grampa said. "Take me—I can predict rain if my old knee hurts."

"Oh, go on, Dave," her gramma chortled.

"I don't want to go back to Washington," Roberta said suddenly. "I want to stay down here."

"Nope. Can't do that." Her grampa shook his head.

"You got a new baby brother or sister to get back to," her gramma reminded her.

Who wants a family with a baby in it? Roberta thought

to herself. It seemed like that baby was always there already, making a mess of everything. If somebody wasn't talking about it, she was thinking about it. She was afraid to tell anyone how much she disliked that baby. She drew in a deep breath.

"Why you so quiet, all at once?" Her gramma asked, looking into her eyes.

"I don't know."

"We got a whole Sunday ahead of us," Gramma Louise said. "They got to put a whole new floor in the church. Won't be no service 'round here till the third Sunday in July. No need to waste time on a sad face."

That night after she had learned to set her alarm, Roberta lay in bed in the lamplight. The day had been good. The three of them were together all day long.

Purple fingertips reminded Roberta of the blackberries she had helped pick from the thorny bushes along the ditch banks on the farm. Gramma had made a pie with strips of flaky crust on top. She was tempted to lick her fingers.

Grampa had invited her to walk with him to look over his cotton and peanut fields. The cornfields were a long ways from the house. "I see a few weeds out here." Grampa trained his eye down the rows of peanuts. "Grass too."

Roberta agreed that she saw a few weeds too, though sometimes she couldn't tell the weeds from the peanut plants. The leaves looked so much alike.

"Think I oughta lay by with the mule and plow tomorrow." Grampa rubbed his chin. "Yep, this here's the last field I got to lay by."

"That's right, Grampa," she said, rubbing her chin, not knowing what he meant about laying by.

"Tomorrow will be a good day," Roberta said to herself now. Her head sank into the feathery pillow. She fell asleep, not knowing when Gramma blew out the lamplight.

Brrrrinnnngggg. The clock sounded like a fire alarm. Roberta jumped out of bed and ran to press the little lever down. Seven o'clock. The weather girl was on the outside of the house.

She hurried to draw the window shade, letting the rising sun into the room. "My weather house works!" she shouted. Not a cloud was in the sky. She could see Grampa Dave in the field with his mule. "I'll eat and feed the chickens," she thought. "Then I'll go in the field with Grampa." She didn't think Gramma would mind.

She was right. Her grandmother was at the front room table, writing something in a thick book.

"I'm going to the peanut field, Gramma," Roberta said politely.

"All right, child." Her gramma smiled but she didn't look up from her work.

The mule was leading the plow and Grampa to the end of the rows when Roberta sat on the ground, three rows away. She didn't like mules much, especially when they hee-hawed like they were hurting.

"Grampa," Roberta yelled. "Are you laying by?"

"Absolutely." Her grandfather pulled on the reins. The mule stopped and waited while Grampa walked over to her and aimed his finger down one row. "See that?"

"See what?"

"That nice dirt the plow laid by the peanut plants. That'll keep the rain from uncovering the roots. Keep weeds and grass off too."

"I see, Grampa," Roberta said. Grampa clicked his tongue and guided the mule to the next row and the next. There was nothing else to see except the blue sky. The sun was getting hot. She decided to go back to the house. It was ten-thirty by the clock when she walked into her room. Her skates stuck out from behind the wardrobe. Quickly, she buckled them on and skated smoothly down the hallway.

"What's all that racket?" her gramma shouted from the front room.

"My skates."

"What?"

"You know—my roller skates."

"Go outdoors with them things, child."

"Yes, ma'am." Roberta skated across the porch and leaped onto the ground. But although she pushed one foot and then the other, she got nowhere. She tried again where the

26

dirt seemed hard. The wheels rotated a couple of times, then nothing but her knees moved. Aching legs made her flop onto the ground. She dragged herself to the chinaberry tree, puffing and sweating.

She hadn't seen them coming, but two strange boys stood there looking down at her. One wore goggles over his eyes and was taller than the other.

"They call me John Allen Superman. This here's my brother. I reckon he's about little as you. We call him Bay Often Ridin' Hay. He likes to ride down hay stacks."

"Those names are not real," Roberta snapped.

"Didn't say so. Said that's what they call us," the taller boy said, bending to spin the wheels of her skates.

"Take your hands off my skates!" Roberta twisted her foot, trying to stand in the soft dirt.

"You talk citified," John Allen said as he straightened up, eyeing one skate and then the other as if he was trying to make up his mind about something. The smaller boy looked at his brother.

"Where do you live?" Roberta asked. She thought she knew where all of the nearby children lived.

"We stayin' with our great aunt. You know her—Miss Ginny. She's old."

"We got down here from Hanover, Virginia, last week," Bay said, eager to join in.

Roberta was full of questions. "Why do you have those

things on your face?" she asked John Allen, thinking the goggles made his face look froggy.

"He gonna fly airplanes," Bay informed her.

"Yep, that's the right way to fly," John Allen said. "These goggles help keep my eyes in practice for rough air."

"He tried to fly off the barn like Superman and he hurt his leg," Bay burst out.

Roberta broke out laughing. "That's why they call you John Allen Superman. You can't fly an airplane either," she snickered.

"Didn't say I could. Said I was going to. B'sides, I jumped off the low shed part of the barn."

"He got pictures and pictures of airplanes at the house." Bay glanced at his brother to see if John Allen was mad at him for telling about how he'd jumped off the barn.

"Want me to show you how to make them things roll good?" John Allen eyed her skates again.

"How? They need a hard surface."

"Give me a day or two to fix 'em up and you'll be flying on them skates," John Allen said, sweeping his hand like an airplane. "The dirt's real hard at the end of the big road."

"Yeah, that's where the pavement runs out," Bay added.

"All right, but you have to give them back in a day or two." Roberta searched for his eyeballs behind the shiny goggles. Deciding that she could trust him, she sat down to unbuckle her new skates.

29

"Hi do, John Allen, Bay," Roberta's grandmother called, greeting the boys from behind the screen door.

"Hi, Miss Louise," they said together.

"Did y'all come to play?" she asked kindly.

"No, ma'am." John Allen shook his head. "I clean forgot! My aunt Ginny said to ask you to send her a pinch of baking soda if you got any, and she said Roberta here"—he looked at Roberta—"can come to play with Lena Mae and them if you have a mind to let her."

"Lena Mae and them?"

"I clean forgot again," John said. "Lena Mae's mama's gone uptown. So her and her brother and sisters gonna stay at my aunt's house till she come back." He took a deep breath.

"Can I go, Gramma?" Roberta pleaded.

"Just for a little while," her gramma allowed. "I'll get the soda."

John Allen carried one skate and Bay carried the other. Roberta carried the soda which felt more like a lump than a pinch. She held the brown wrapping carefully as they took the shortcut over the thick planks of wood that crossed a stream of water and followed along the head row of the cotton field. They ended up in Miss Ginny's backyard. John Allen and Bay disappeared behind the barn.

Lena Mae ran and joined hands with Roberta. "Hey, Roberta. Did you come to play?" she asked eagerly.

"Yes," Roberta said, feeling welcomed.

"We heard you got here yesterday," Lena May said, skipping off. "Everybody round front looking for you— come on."

Roberta's heart raced. They were all waiting for *her*.

Lena Mae's sister Dewildera ran to the porch, leading four barefooted children from where they had been playing. Jimmy and Janey were twins. They were younger than Lena Mae. Sadie was younger than the twins. Harriet was the youngest of all. They all said, "Hey."

Miss Ginny was holding a baby. "What a blessing to lay eyes on you again," the old woman said with a smile, leaning over from her porch swing to accept the baking soda. "What a blessing."

"Thank you, ma'am" Roberta said thoughtfully. Miss Ginny's tiny plaits were wrapped in white twine, the same color as her hair. Where did she get that baby from? Roberta wondered. She couldn't take her eyes off him.

"Roberta came to play," Dewildera said to the others. She was eleven and the oldest. "Y'all come on."

chapter four

As they all joined hands to form a ring, John Allen and Bay ran over to take part in the game. Roberta wondered what they had done with her skates.

"Lena Mae, you be it first this time," Dewildera said. Everybody laughed when Lena Mae stood in the middle of the ring. Slowly, the children stepped sideways and the ring moved in the direction of a clock hand.

Lena Mae walked in a small circle within the ring in the opposite direction. She eyed the clamped hands.

"Better watch out for her," Janey warned, squeezing Roberta's hand.

"Yep, better watch out," John Allen added.

Two or three times, Lena Mae sang like she was sad.

I smell my mama's biscuits burning—

Two or three times, the children answered like they were mad.

Don't care, ya can't get outta here!

Lena Mae sang again.

I must get home before the sun goes down—

Roberta giggled along with the others as Lena Mae widened her circle within the ring, coming closer to them.

Don't care, ya can't get outa here!

The larger circle stopped. Roberta followed their lead as they pressed against each other to keep Lena Mae from escaping the ring.

I hear my mama calling my name—

Suddenly, Roberta didn't know what to do next. Lena Mae was standing right in front of her, staring.

"Don't let her out," they all warned. "Hold hands tight!"

Lena Mae didn't pay them no mind. She sang like she was really sad this time.

I'll break my neck into twenty-five pieces—

Lena Mae took something from her pocket and turned to the other side of the ring.

"Hey, Lena Mae," John Allen shouted, dropping hands. "Over here! Watch out, Roberta!"

Don't care ya can't get outa here!

Before Roberta could even think about it, Lena Mae whirled around and poked a feather under her nose. It didn't take but a split second to rub the itchy feeling away, but a split second was all the time Lena Mae needed to break out of the ring and sing as she ran.

I said it, I meant it, I elbow bent it
If you wanta get mad about it
Step back in it!

The ring broke into running feet. "Catch her!" they all shouted. Roberta ran faster than the younger children did. John Allen and Bay passed her by but Dewildera was the only one fast enough to catch Lena Mae before the younger girl reached a big pine tree. They sat on the ground, laughing and puffing for breath.

"I told y'all to watch out for Lena Mae," John Allen said to Roberta.

"I didn't know she was going to tickle my nose." Roberta gave Lena Mae a how-could-you-do-that-to-me look.

"Can't nobody keep me in the ring, I don't care how much y'all watch out," Lena Mae teased.

Roberta took off her shoes and poured out the loose, dark brown sand that had gotten into them as she played. "I want to be it next," she said above the chatter.

"You have to catch the runner first, then you can be it," Dewildera told her.

"I'll never be it," Roberta said to herself, knowing she couldn't outrun Dewildera. "No fair." She peeled off her sweaty socks and stuffed them into her shoes.

"De-wil-dera," Miss Ginny called, her voice cracking.

"Ma'am?" Dewildera answered.

"Come see 'bout this baby!" Miss Ginny answered.

"Our baby must be crying," Dewildera said, starting toward the house. "Y'all come on back to the house," she directed without a backward glance.

Roberta trotted along with the others, carrying her shoes. The spongy earth squashed between her toes. By the time they reached the house, Miss Ginny was sitting on the porch swing, patting the squalling baby. "Don't you cry—she comin'," the old woman cooed to the baby as Dewildera went inside.

"Where did Dewildera go?" Roberta asked, not wanting their play to end. She placed her shoes on the steps and moved closer to the swing. "What's the matter?"

"Babies cry," John Allen said simply. He and Bay sat on the steps with Jimmy and the sisters.

All at once, Dewildera hurried from behind the door with milk in a bottle. The squalling stopped as soon as she cradled the little head in her arms. She sat in the swing beside Miss Ginny and put the bottle nipple in the infant's mouth.

"He wouldn't take that bottle from me," Miss Ginny said, smiling when she saw the milk bubbles form at the neck of the bottle. "He wanted his big sister."

So the baby was Lena Mae's new brother, Roberta thought. She had never been so close to a baby this small. Miss Ginny had said "he." Roberta wouldn't have been able to tell on her own if it was a boy or a girl. "How old is he?" She touched the little arm.

"Four months," Dewildera said, moving the baby out of her reach.

"You been playin' in dirt," Miss Ginny said kindly. "Got to have clean hands to touch little babies."

"Yes, ma'am." Roberta quickly wiped her hands on her dress and reached for the baby's fingers.

"I said *clean* hands," Miss Ginny said firmly.

Roberta snatched her hand back and turned away. Her face felt hot. She didn't feel like playing anymore. She wanted to talk to Gramma. By the time she retrieved her shoes, the boys had disappeared. Lena Mae was playing a string game with her sisters.

"Wanta play some more?" her friend asked, looking up.

"I have to go home now," Roberta said. "Gramma said I couldn't play but a little while."

"I'll walk a piece of the way with you." Lena Mae jumped to her feet, shedding the strings into Sadie's lap.

"Just a piece of the way," Miss Ginny called out, having overheard. "And Little Miss Roberta, you tell your grandma I said much obliged for the baking soda."

"Yes, ma'am." Roberta grabbed Lena Mae's hand and dashed around the corner of the porch. They headed along the path toward the stream.

"Wait on," Lena Mae complained, pulling back. "Piece of the way will be gone in no time the way you running."

"I want to get away from Miss Ginny," Roberta said, slowing to a walk.

"What did she do?"

"I don't know," Roberta grumbled. She thought about asking about Lena Mae's baby brother, but something inside wouldn't let her. The fact that Dewildera had said "our baby" put questions in her mind too. The little arm felt soft, not stiff like her baby dolls. Then Dewildera had moved the baby away and Miss Ginny had acted like Roberta was dirty.

"You think you can come to play tomorrow?" Lena Mae asked. "Maybe my mama will let me come to your house. Or maybe you can come to my house. We won't be at Miss Ginny's tomorrow."

Roberta answered, "I don't know" and "I might" to the questions. Though they walked slowly the stream crossed the path in no time.

Lena Mae sat on the boards and sank her feet ankle deep into the clear water.

Roberta sat beside her friend, keeping her feet dry. She watched the water flow over large stepping-stones. The stream wandered through a cluster of reeds and bushes and then it went on, out of sight. A minute or so passed while her friend sloshed her feet around. "Lena Mae, do you like babies?"

"They all right," her friend said, kicking water into the air.

"A new baby's coming to my house in Washington."

"That's good." Cold water splashed higher.

"That is *not* good!" Roberta jumped up, wiping water off of her legs.

"'Scuse me." Lena Mae quickly swung her dripping feet around and stood up. "I didn't mean to wet you up." She studied her wet footprints on the smooth boards.

"Miss Ginny might think you walked me all the way home," Roberta warned, hoping Lena Mae would start back.

"No, she won't."

"Well, I have to go—see you tomorrow." Roberta sped off down the narrow path, not used to her bare feet pounding on the small stones and twigs.

"Tomorrow!" Lena Mae yelled.

"Okay!" Roberta shouted back. Now if she could just make it to Gramma, that sad feeling would go away. She ran on past the trail to Mister Joe Baker's hog pen and over the head rows of somebody's field of peanuts.

"Stop running so in this heat," Roberta heard her gramma yell from the porch. Roberta didn't stop until she was in her gramma's lap, crying and gulping for air.

"Stop that fuss and tell me what ails you," her gramma said, trying to shush her.

"I don't know," Roberta blurted out.

"Did you play with Lena Mae and them?"

"Yes, ma'am." Roberta hiccuped, tugging gramma's heavy arm around her.

"Did you have a good time?"

"Yes, ma'am."

"What made you cry?"

"Miss Ginny said I had dirty hands."

"How come?"

"I touched that little ugly baby."

"Ohh, Roberta," her gramma said. "You mad?"

"Yes, ma'am." Roberta wiped her face with her hands. Gramma's lap rocked back and forth. "Do you want to ask me some more questions?" Roberta asked, looking into her gramma's eyes.

"I'm wonderin' what you mad about, child," Gramma said, still rocking.

"Well, I don't want to play at Miss Ginny's house no more," Roberta said with dry eyes.

"What y'all play?"

"We played a game where you sing, '*I smell my mama's biscuits burning.*'" Her voice carried the tune. Roberta laughed then, thinking about Lena Mae's feather.

"Your daddy used to play that ring game." Gramma looked like she was seeing a long ways back.

"He did?" Roberta asked, surprised.

"Shore did."

In her mind's eye, Roberta could see her daddy as a boy, the size of John Allen, playing a trick to keep someone inside the ring. His pranks always made her laugh.

"Hey, heah!" Grampa said, breaking them out of their thoughts. He climbed onto the other side of the porch. "Where's dinner?"

"In the kitchen, Dave," her gramma said with a laugh. "Be ready soon."

"You almost scared me," Roberta joked. She slipped off her gramma's lap. "You're just like Daddy."

"Your daddy's just like me," he said. "I'm the oldest."

"Oh, that's right," Roberta said, following her grandparents inside to wash her hands.

At the dinner table, she asked Grampa if he played ring games when he was a boy.

"We played so many of 'em," He said, biting into a hot biscuit. "But if you talkin' 'bout the ones that say *put your hands on your hips and let your backbone slip,* I didn't play it."

"Boys didn't play such games—that was for girls," Gramma explained, dipping the last of the butterbeans out of her best bowl.

"How do you make your backbone slip?" Roberta wanted to know. "I bet Dewildera can show me," she added, eyeing the empty bowl. Her stomach was full, but she scraped little bits of meat from the ham bone anyway.

Grampa tilted his glass to drink the last swallow of water.

"Good dinner, good dinner," he said to Gramma as he left the kitchen. Laying by was on his mind.

"What does he have to do after he lay by?" Roberta asked as she carefully laid the plates in the dishpan.

"Rest up and watch everything grow. He might finish up today," Gramma said.

That would make Gramma happy, Roberta thought. She spent the rest of the day helping Gramma work in the house and garden. The baby crossed her mind a few times, but she didn't tell Gramma about it. She almost wanted to see him again when she thought about how tiny his toenails and fingernails looked—like little dots.

 chapter five

Tuesday morning when the alarm sounded, the little old man with the umbrella was standing outside the weather house. Roberta heard the raindrops sprinkling the rooftop. She raised the shade. Drizzling rain made the fields dull and soggy.

After breakfast, Grampa sat in the hallway, whittling. Wood shavings danced around before landing onto an old sheet he had laid on the floor. Gramma sat in their bedroom, sewing together cutout squares.

"What can I do?" Roberta asked Gramma.

"I want to make us some good hot barbecue for supper. Go see if Miss Mabel can send me a few bolls of hot pepper."

"Yes, ma'am! Can I stay for a little while too?"

"If Miss Mabel let y'all play in the house—just a little while," Gramma said, handing Roberta an old umbrella from the corner of the room.

"Hmm! I heard somebody say barbecue," Grampa said over his pile of wood shavings.

"Don't play too long—behave yourself."

"Yes, Grampa." Roberta smiled and headed for the front porch. After several starts, the umbrella clicked and stayed up. She balanced the handle across her shoulder and stepped into the rain and onto the sand-crusted roadway. Miss Mabel's house was in the opposite direction from Miss Ginny's. She decided not to try and touch that little baby when she got to Lena Mae's house—won't even look at him, she thought. She decided that she would ask Dewildera to show her the game about how to make your backbone slip.

Soon the familiar, gray two-story house stood up from the bottom of the road, in the middle of fields the same as surrounded all of the other houses. A big oak tree squatted near a small garden. Its branches spanned half of the yard and reached above the housetop. Someone had built a new bench around the trunk. A swing hung from one of the limbs.

"Well, Roberta!" Miss Mabel answered Roberta's knock with a wide smile. "We heard you gonna be down here in the country for a good while—hi you doin'?"

"Fine, thank you," Roberta said. She entered the foyer and tilted the closed umbrella against the wall, looking up the stairway.

"Roberta! Did you come to play?" A delighted Lena Mae suddenly emerged from the front room to the left of the stairway.

"Yes," Roberta answered happily, "but I have to ask Miss Mabel something first." She looked up at Lena Mae's mother, who was taller than Gramma but not as wide. "Gramma said send her a few bolls of hot pepper and I can play in the house for a little while if you let me." Roberta crossed her fingers.

"All right. Y'all play a little while, then I'll let you have the pepper," Miss Mabel said, walking upstairs.

"Where's Dewildera and them?" Roberta asked.

"Upstairs. The mailman brought us a wish book—a good one too!"

"Wish book?" Roberta asked, following Lena Mae into the front room where a large, brown settee claimed most of the space. A thick catalog and a pair of scissors lay open on the floor.

"See?" Lena Mae cradled the book in her lap and motioned for Roberta to sit beside her.

"Oh, a catalog," Roberta said as Lena Mae flipped pages showing girls their age wearing pretty dresses.

"It's a wish book," Lena Mae insisted. "See anything you wish for?"

All of the little girls in the catalog had happy faces and matching shoes. Some wore hats and ribbons in their hair. This was fun. Roberta pointed to one of the models, thinking of her dress hanging in Gramma's wardrobe. "How do you like that one?"

"I don't." Lena Mae glanced at the ruffled blue dress. "Mama said it's too hard to iron."

"Well, I wish for that one." Roberta pointed to a pale green dress with puffed sleeves and a white collar. The girl held a jacket that went with it. A smaller picture showed how the front and back of the jacket looked.

"That's pretty," Lena Mae remarked, carefully tearing the page away from the book's spine. "Here, you can cut it out." She handed Roberta a scissors.

"Your mother might get mad."

"No, she won't." Lena Mae scanned a few more pages. "It's my turn to pick out of this wish book before anybody else—this is the one I like!" She traced her finger over a fluffy pink dress. The scooped neck was embroidered with flowers.

"That's the prettiest one," Roberta observed, wishing she had seen the dress first.

"I can see me sashaying." Lena Mae swayed like she was the girl with bows on her shoulders.

"Tear it out," Roberta urged so that she could find another pretty dress.

Several wish-book dresses lined the settee when Dewildera walked into the room. "What y'all doing?"

"Dewildera, look at our dresses—which one you like the best?" Lena Mae led her oldest sister to the settee.

"All of 'em pretty," Dewildera said, looking long at a blue

velvet dress that had a round collar. She turned to leave the room, motioning for them to retrieve their dresses. "Y'all need some paste."

"For what?" Roberta inquired as she carefully picked up her five cutouts and followed the others into the kitchen.

"We gonna stick our dresses on some stiff-back paper, like dolls," Lena Mae informed Roberta at the kitchen table.

Dewildera scooped flour into a mixing bowl, added water, and stirred the mixture into a creamy paste.

Roberta didn't think the flour paste would be sticky enough, but it was. In about fifteen minutes, nine wish-book dolls stood upright on a cardboard base Dewildera had made. Dewildera can do anything, Roberta thought as the older girl folded newspaper around her dolls and placed them into a sack so that Roberta could take them home.

Just then, Roberta heard the baby's irritating cry.

"I gotta get him 'cause Mama's fixing my skirt," Dewildera said as she rushed out of the kitchen.

Lena Mae folded her arms around her group of dolls. "All these dresses are mine to wish for," she bragged. "Which one of yours you wish for the most, Roberta?"

"I wish that baby—" Roberta closed her lips before she said something she shouldn't.

"What 'bout the baby?" Lena Mae asked.

"Roberta?" Miss Mabel called, entering the kitchen. "I got the pepper ready for you."

"Yes, ma'am," Roberta said, glad to take the little bag of pepper from Miss Mabel and say her goodbyes. She didn't want to think about that baby.

The rain spattered the top of the umbrella now. Roberta walked fast, thinking about how close she had come to telling Lena Mae that what she really wished for was not in a catalog.

Then she remembered she didn't have the chance to ask about the make-your-backbone-slip game.

"Mabel sent me more than enough," said Gramma when she looked inside the bag of peppers.

"What's that you got, child?" Grampa asked her from the rocking chair.

"Wish-book dresses," Roberta said, opening the sack so that he and Gramma could see.

Nice," they said. She entered her room and arranged her dolls on the bureau. "I wish that baby in Mama's stomach . . . I wish—," Roberta tried to say what she was feeling. She couldn't.

"Want to ride with Grampa to get fresh meat for the barbecue, Roberta?" Gramma asked from the doorway.

"No, thank you." Roberta heard the truck cough and sneeze. "That's an ugly old truck."

"Was that the right thing to say?" Gramma asked firmly.

"No, ma'am."

"Well?"

"Well, I'm going to write a letter to Mama." Roberta pushed past Gramma and headed for the front room.

"Not yet. Come back here and talk to me first. What you mad about?" Gramma asked.

"Nothing, I'm not mad."

"Go ahead and write to your mama then," Gramma said with a sigh.

For a long time, Roberta sat at the table, trying to think of how to spell the words she really wanted to write. Beating rain on the roof didn't help her concentration. She finally got the words down.

Dear Mama,

I am fine. I hope you are fine too. It is raining down here.

Grampa can not work in the fild. I said a bad thing about his truck. I said I was sory. I am a good girl. I played with Lena Mae.

Gramma is fine. She is making somthing.

I fed chikins today. I hope you are not sick. Tell Daddy I said hello. I love you. I love Daddy.

Yours truely,

Roberta

"There," she said, feeling better after reading the letter several times. "I spelled all of my words correct." She placed the letter on her bureau.

The rain really poured Wednesday, the next day. Roberta couldn't mail her letter. Grampa's truck wouldn't start. "Wet wires," he said. So there she was, stuck in the house again with nothing to do for three more days.

That Saturday morning, Roberta didn't know what awakened her first—the alarm clock or the bright sunshine. The little girl stood on the porch of the weather house. Roberta couldn't get dressed fast enough. "I have to mail my letter," she said, flying into the room to check the envelope before sealing the flap.

"Want me to look it over?" Gramma offered.

"I know how to write," Roberta said from her room. She heard her grandparents chuckle.

"Well, you gonna have to stand at the mailbox and buy a stamp. Mailman will come by 'round nine-thirty this morning."

"I know how." Roberta smiled from her bedroom doorway. "It's fifteen minutes past nine by my clock."

They chuckled again.

Grampa met her in the hallway and dug in his pocket. "Here's some money for stamps." He dropped a dime and two pennies in her hand. "Put one stamp on your letter and bring three stamps back," he told her.

"Thank you, Grampa." She walked briskly down the dirt road, taking care to hop over the puddles of water. She skirted around the puddles that were big enough for her to see her reflection.

Six mailboxes clustered along the paved road not far from Miss Ginny's house. Cars were driving by. Roberta found the box that said, "Dave Robinson, Box 49, Scotland Neck, N.C." That was the same address her mother and father wrote to. Now she was writing from the same address.

There were no houses on the other side of the paved road, just fields of corn that went on and on. Roberta walked on the shoulder of the road, just in front of the mailboxes, straining to see the end of the tassled stalks.

Three short beeps of a horn startled her, and she pressed

up against the mailboxes to get out of the way, her heart beating fast.

"Good morning." The mailman spoke sharply.

"Good morning." Roberta spoke with a shaky voice.

He leaned toward her from the driver's seat. Neatly wrapped packages, bundles of letters, and newspapers were stacked around him. "You mailing something?"

"Yes." She handed him the money and the letter. "I want to buy stamps with the rest of the money."

"Alrighty." He looked at her letter and tore off three extra stamps. "Here's mail for the Robinson box." He handed her a newspaper with the letters and stamps. "Next time, little girl, don't stand in front of the mailboxes."

The car tires kicked back shoulder dirt and sped down the paved road before Roberta could say, "I'm not little." She glanced down at the letters. The one on top was addressed to Dave Robinson. The other said, *Miss Roberta Robinson*. "I got a letter from Mama!" she shouted, and sat on the damp ground, ripping the envelope open. Her fingers unfolded a whole page in perfect school-book print.

My dear Roberta,

Your daddy brought your sweet letter home to me. I am doing fine. He said to tell his baby girl hello. He and Aunt Emma are taking good care of me.

I am making baby clothes and counting the days.
When you get this letter I will have three weeks
left to wait. Then your daddy and I will have two
children. Don't you think that is nice? All of us
will be so happy.

 Make sure you do your part and help Gramma
Louise and Grampa Dave. I know you are enjoying
yourself. Your daddy and I miss you. This is all
for now.

I love you.
Mama

Three weeks, Roberta thought, folding the letter and stuffing it into the torn envelope. She walked toward Gramma's house slowly.

She sloshed through every puddle in her path. Everybody was getting ready for that baby. Aunt Emma was still bragging about the "new baby" in the family, Roberta guessed. Her daddy acted like he could hardly wait. "I spend the time making baby clothes," she quoted her mama's words out loud. Roberta squeezed the letter tightly. She suddenly wanted to tear it into little bitty pieces.

Gramma and Grampa were sitting on the porch, snapping beans.

"This is for you, Grampa," she said as she handed him his mail.

He took the letter and newspaper, watching her carefully.

Roberta walked past them into her room. Gramma tip-toed in and found her lying on the bed. The sticky stamps were on the pillow.

"Don't you want to get some nice sunshine, child?"

"No, ma'am."

"Mailman give you a letter for yourself?"

"Yes, ma'am—from Mama." Roberta pulled the crinkled page out of the envelope and laid it on the bed. "You can read it." She buried her face in the pillow.

In a little while, Gramma said, "My, my" and "Ain't that good."

The inside of Roberta's stomach began to tremble. She hated that feeling. It could mean she was about to lose her breakfast.

"Well, get up. I got to ride uptown and get groceries . . . pay insurance . . . get something from the Five-and-Dime store . . . and pay money on that suit Pittman's is holding for your grampa," Gramma said, as if she was reading from a long list.

"Here come somebody!" Grampa yelled from the porch.

Roberta ran to the window. "It's Lena Mae," she said, surprised.

"Go out there, child," Gramma said encouragingly.

"Hi, Lena Mae." Roberta ran to welcome her friend at the chinaberry tree.

"Hey, Roberta." Lena Mae was grinning.

"Did you come to play?" Roberta asked.

"Yeah." Lena Mae grabbed Roberta's hands and they spun around.

"Gramma!" Roberta yelled the tremble out of her stomach. "Lena Mae came to play!"

Gramma came to the door. "We have to go uptown, you know."

"Roberta can stay at our house till y'all come back," Lena Mae said.

"Mabel know 'bout this?" Gramma asked.

"No, ma'am, but I can ask her."

"Can I go?" Roberta danced up and down.

"What you think, Dave?" Gramma asked Grampa.

"We'll stop by Mabel's and tell her what time we expect to come home. Let her go."

As soon as Roberta and Lena Mae heard the word *go*, they sped off.

"Behave yourself," Gramma yelled after them.

"I'm a good girl!" Roberta shouted, not turning around.

chapter six

Miss Mabel was hanging clothes on the line in the backyard. A big wooden washtub and scrub board rested on a bench near the well.

"Hi, Miss Mabel," Roberta called.

"Hey there, Roberta!" Miss Mabel smiled. Her apron was wet from bending over the washtub. "I thought you and Lena Mae were playin' at your gramma's house."

Roberta let Lena Mae cut in to explain about Gramma and Grampa going uptown.

"Of course it's all right with me," Miss Mabel said, shaking a blouse from her basket of wet clothes. "Go play."

The two girls chatted on their way across the yard and through the back door.

"Roberta's here!" Jimmy called upstairs as soon as they walked in.

In a twinkling, all except Dewildera ran bumpety-bumpety down the steps.

"I came to play!" Roberta explained. "Where's Dewildera?"

"Tending to the baby," Harriet said.

"Come on, let's play in the shade, out front." Jimmy inched nearer to the door. "Last one out is a stinking skunk."

Roberta held back as everybody raced toward the door. She wanted to ask Dewildera about how to make a backbone slip. But Lena Mae doubled back.

"You gonna be the stinking skunk!" Lena Mae poked her head through the door, snickering.

"I want to see Dewildera about something first," Roberta said, heading up the steps.

"What for?"

Roberta couldn't explain. Somehow, she knew that Dewildera would not laugh at her questions. Something inside made her want to see that baby again too. So she kept climbing until she reached the top of the stairs.

"Dewildera," Roberta called softly.

"In here." Dewildera's voice came from the end room. "Is that you, Roberta?"

"Yes." Roberta entered a bedroom that smelled of sweet powder. "I want to ask you something."

"Wait till I change the baby," Dewildera managed to say with two big safety pins sticking out of the side of her mouth. The baby was lying on a blanket across the big bed.

Roberta watched the wiggling baby for a minute. "What's his name?"

"Sterling Henry Johnson," Dewildera said, fastening the

triangular diaper together. "He's named after our daddy. We call him Junior."

"Where's your daddy?" In all of her short visits, Roberta had never seen a daddy there.

"He went back to Richmond yesterday," Dewildera said proudly. "That's where he works most of the time. We're saving money for us to buy this house and land we live on."

"Oh," said Roberta. Dewildera pinned a strip of white cloth around the baby's stomach.

"What's that?" Roberta asked, careful not to touch the baby as she pointed at the cloth.

"His belly band. He got to wear this till his little back grow strong."

"Oh."

Junior jabbered and poked his fist into his mouth. "May I hold him if I wash my hands?" Roberta didn't know what had made her ask.

"You don't know how to hold no baby."

"Yes I do. I'll hold him just like you." Roberta took tiny breaths as she waited for a response.

Dewildera frowned. Gently, she pulled a shirtsleeve up the baby's arm, then up the other arm. Little buttons had to be fastened.

Finally she looked at Roberta. "Go down to the kitchen," she directed, "where the wash-pan stand is. There's some soap there and a dipper and—"

"I know what to do," Roberta broke in, rushing but not running out of the room. Within a few seconds, she was in the kitchen.

The wash pan, soap, and the bucket of water were next to the window, like at Gramma's house. Two dippers full of water were enough, she thought. Hastily, she scrubbed and dried her hands on a spotless towel that draped from a homemade rack, like at Gramma's house too.

Dewildera was holding the baby on her shoulder when Roberta entered the room for the second time.

"See, I washed my hands clean," Roberta said when she returned, spreading her fingers for Dewildera to inspect.

"Sit down." Dewildera motioned to a slat-back chair.

Keeping her eyes on the baby, Roberta almost missed the seat. "I'm sitting down." She held her arms out.

"Move your arms out'n the way," Dewildera said quietly. "I'm gonna put him on your lap."

Roberta took a deep breath.

"Now you're holding the baby," Dewildera said, letting go.

"I know." Roberta wrapped her arms around his little waist.

As quick as a wink, that baby threw his head against Roberta's chest, flailed every limb on his little body, and let out a cry loud enough to make her want to push him onto the floor.

"Junior, Junior," Dewildera cooed, quickly lifting the baby away. "Don't cry—I got you."

The baby stopped crying and laid his head on Dewildera's shoulder.

After a little while, Roberta asked, "Lena Mae ever hold the baby?"

"Lots of times. Jimmy and Janey too."

"I don't like babies," Roberta said, standing up.

"Why?"

"Because babies don't like me." She squared her shoulders and stomped toward the door.

"You don't mean that," Dewildera said. "What did you want to ask me?"

"Nothing." Roberta ran down the steps and through the front door, pushing the baby's cry from her mind.

"Roberta, we need you to be the needle with me," Lena Mae shouted from the shady oak.

The invitation sounded like music to Roberta. They needed her. She hop-skipped over to the group. "Do you all know how to make your backbone slip?" she dared to blurt out.

"Not me," Jimmy scoffed. "You're talking 'bout Here Come Uncle Jesse. Girls play that ol' game. I wanna play Grandma Gonna Thread My Needle, like we said before." Jimmy sounded mad.

"Well, Roberta *is* company." Lena Mae reminded her younger brother that it was impolite not to let company choose first.

"Yeah, Jimmy," Janey fussed at her twin brother. "We can change the game if we want to."

"Yeah, Jimmy," Sadie and Harriet echoed.

"No fair!" Jimmy shouted.

"I don't care what we play," Roberta yelled when he shouted in her face. "I don't care!"

"Hey, Hey!" Dewildera appeared in the yard—from no-where, it seemed to Roberta. "I heard everything," she said to stop the fighting. To Roberta, it seemed like Dewildera was always there, taking care of the baby, leading the games; now her sisters and brother gathered around her, listening.

Roberta stood outside the circle, wishing.

"You started Grandma Gonna Thread My Needle, so go on and finish it. *Then* play Uncle Jesse. Then, Jimmy, you come inside, 'cause I got something for boys to do." Dewildera headed for the door.

"Aw, you not gonna play?" Jimmy whined after his oldest sister.

"Nope. After I finish my work I'm gonna make me some cookies." She went through the doorway.

"You said I was going to be the needle with you, Lena

Mae," Roberta said, relieved that no one was mad anymore. "What do I do?"

"Wait," Jimmy said. "First you and Lena Mae have to choose us."

Lena Mae led Roberta into the hot sun. "Which do you like the best—cake or ice cream?" Lena Mae whispered.

Roberta remembered the taste of Aunt Emma's coconut cake. "Cake."

"All right. I like ice cream," Lena Mae said, pleased. "Now, when the ones we catch say they like ice cream the best, they'll stand behind me."

"And if they like cake the best, they'll stand behind me," Roberta said. "But how do we catch them?"

"That's easy. Let's go." They ran back to the shade where Jimmy and his sisters lined up, one behind the other.

Lena Mae joined hands with Roberta to form an archway. "This is the eye of the needle," Lena Mae explained.

"What do we do now?" Roberta asked.

Jimmy gave his "she's so pitiful" laugh.

"Listen to me sing and then you join in," Lena Mae encouraged, ignoring Jimmy. "When I give you the signal like this"—she squeezed Roberta's hand—"we bring our arms down and catch the ones going through the needle, like thread."

"I have it!" Roberta almost jumped for joy. She watched

the children file through the eye of the needle that she helped to make. The singing started.

Grandma gonna thread my needle—so low, so low
Grandma gonna thread my needle—so high

When Roberta joined in, Sadie, Harriet, and Janey stopped short of the needle, not knowing when the signal would be given. Then they ran through as fast as they could.

My thread got a great big knot in it—so low, so low
My thread got a great big knot in it—so high

Jimmy strutted through, daring them to catch him. On his fifth time around the ring, Lena Mae signaled Roberta. Their arms came crashing down. Jimmy ducked to his knees and scrambled out of their reach.

The giggly younger girls were easy to catch. One by one Roberta and Lena Mae took them aside to have them choose between ice cream and cake. Finally, Jimmy was caught.

At the end, three children stood behind Roberta. Jimmy and Lena Mae were the only ones who liked ice cream best.

"I won, didn't I?" Roberta asked, not sure.

"Hah!" Jimmy said.

"Now we have to see which side is the strongest," Lena

Mae said, drawing a line on the ground with her finger. Sadie ran to retrieve a rope from the tree bench.

"Four against two," Jimmy said, sure that he and Lena Mae could win the tug of war. "Four little weaklings. Let me in front, Lena Mae. We'll pull all of them across the line."

"We're going to win, Jimmy, and you can't do anything about it." Roberta laid her belief on thick. She held one end of the rope, leaving enough slack for Sadie, Janey, and Harriet to grab. Jimmy did the same for Lena Mae.

"One, two," Jimmy counted rapidly. On the count of three he yanked with all his might, catching everyone off guard.

Roberta's foot slid close to the line. "Pull," she yelled, twisting her face into a knot.

"Look at her," Jimmy teased. "Weakling." He leaned forward, snickering.

As he did, Roberta leaned back with all her body weight.

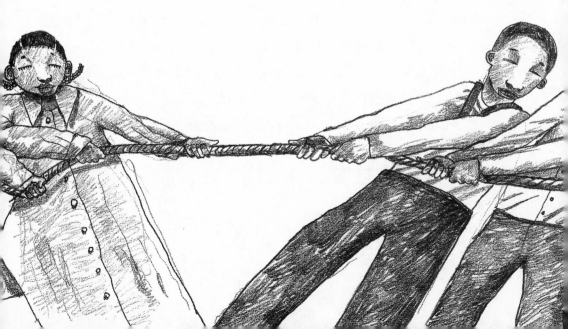

Jimmy's foot slid toward the line.

"Pull, Jimmy, pull!" Lena Mae instructed her giggling brother.

"I have to win," Roberta thought. "Pull! Pull!" she yelled.

Jimmy released the rope when his big toe inched across the line, spilling everybody onto the ground.

"My side won!" Roberta shouted. "My side won!"

"Oh, I just let you win," Jimmy scoffed.

"We won, fair and square," Roberta said, sure of herself.

"Fair and square," they yelled, circling Jimmy until he ran into the house to escape them.

"Here come Miss Louise and Mister Dave," Janey announced from the tree bench.

"My side won," Roberta ran to say when the truck idled to a stop.

"Y'all gedown and come in," Miss Mabel called from the doorway. She was holding the baby now.

"No, we thank you." Gramma poked her head out of the window. "We just dropped by to let you know we'll finish uptown about an hour or so from now."

"The girls told me all 'bout it." Miss Mabel nodded.

"My side won," Roberta said again, clapping.

"Much obliged," Grampa said, backing the rattling truck out of the yard.

"That's good, child," Gramma praised Roberta. "Real good."

Roberta waved until the truck turned up the road. Soon it would reach the paved road that would take Gramma and Grampa to the town of Scotland Neck. She would not have traded going uptown with them for being on the winning side.

chapter seven

"I bet y'all don't know what I'm doing," Jimmy called from the doorway.

"I know I won, Jimmy," Roberta said, but he had ducked back into the house. They lazed on the tree bench, no one talking. She decided not to say anything about the Uncle Jesse game until after dinner. Thinking about how her team had beat the other side was wonderful.

Shady breezes dried their sweaty bodies and brought the smell of ginger and molasses to their noses. Dewildera's cookies, Roberta thought.

After a while, Lena Mae stood in the bright sunshine. "If I can step on the head part of my shadow"—Lena Mae took a tiny step—"it's about twelve o'clock and time for dinner."

"Is that true?" Roberta jumped into the hot sun and stepped on her head shadow.

"Y'all get washed for dinner," Jimmy called just then.

"Wait until I tell Gramma I can tell time without a clock," Roberta said, laughing.

"She know that," Lena Mae chuckled, leading the line of them inside the house and to the washstand.

Miss Mabel and Dewildera were busy forking salmon cakes, finely chopped collard greens, and steamed rice on the plates. This was Roberta's first time eating at Lena Mae's house.

"Y'all hurry up," Jimmy urged from his seat at the head of the table. He kept his eye on the bar of soap that slipped through four-year-old Harriet's hand. "Let me help you out," he said, rushing to lift his little sister within reach of the wash pan.

"I can wash my hands by myself, Jimmy," Harriet declared loudly. "Put me down!"

Roberta took a chair beside Lena Mae. Janey and Sadie shared a bench on the other side of the table. Jimmy dried Harriet's hands. Then he watched her climb onto a chair that had a block of wood on the seat so that she would be even with the table.

Dewildera placed a dish of chopped onions and a plate of sliced tomatoes in the middle of the table.

"Let's us sit down, Dewildera," Miss Mabel said, looking at Harriet's frowning face.

Roberta laughed when Harriet folded her hands and closed her eyes like the picture of an angel when her brother bowed his head to say grace.

As soon as Jimmy said amen he told them, "Don't take so

long to eat; I got something to show y'all." He put a fork full of collard greens into his mouth.

"And I got something to show too, Jimmy," Miss Mabel said. "I'm gonna wait till everybody's done taking their time to eat. If I can wait, you can wait."

The table turned into eaters, not talkers. Roberta thought Miss Mabel's cooking tasted as good as Gramma's. She sprinkled some onions on her collards.

"I don't eat raw onions," Janey announced.

"I don't eat raw tomatoes," Sadie quickly added.

Dewildera chuckled and reached for second helpings of tomatoes and onions. "Taste good to me."

Jimmy sighed, looking at Harriet, the slowest eater.

She had trouble picking up several grains of scattered rice with her fork. Jimmy looked like he wanted to help her out again. Finally, she used her fingers and picked them up one by one until they were gone.

"Good for Harriet," Dewildera said, clapping.

Roberta joined in as the others applauded, thinking, Why clap for someone who does not know how to use a fork? There wasn't one speck of food left on her own plate, and she hadn't used her fingers.

"Now I can show y'all," Jimmy said happily.

"Let Mama be first," Janey intoned, cutting her eye at Jimmy.

"Naw, naw," Miss Mabel said.

"I made something for everybody here," Jimmy explained gleefully. "You have to find it though. I'll tell you if you're hot or cold."

Roberta scraped her seat away from the table as fast as the rest of them.

"Can I play?" Dewildera teased.

"Naw, you and Mama can't be in it, Dewildera!" Jimmy exclaimed. "Y'all know already."

"Where is it, Jimmy?" Harriet whispered in Jimmy's ear.

"You have to find it," Jimmy said, to Harriet's disappointment.

"Over here?" Roberta asked, moving near the washstand.

"Cold as ice," Jimmy said with a laugh.

Janey and Sadie dawdled into the hallway.

"Cold." Jimmy was having the most fun.

"Let's stay together," Lena Mae suggested after Jimmy had yelled "cold" as they looked around the settee, under the tables, and behind the curtains in the front room. They rushed into the kitchen.

"Cold!" Jimmy yelled.

"I can't find it," Harriet said sadly. She left the group and leaned against the cupboard on the back wall.

"Hot!" Jimmy yelled.

"Slow down," Miss Mabel cautioned as the children crowded around the tables and chairs near the still-hot woodstove.

Roberta opened the cupboard's bottom doors—nothing there but plates, cups, and saucers. They could see through the upper glass doors—nothing there but Miss Mabel's best water pitchers and glasses.

"There it is," Roberta pointed at the fringe of tea towels hanging over the top of the cupboard.

"You found it!" Jimmy cheered.

"Y'all let me take it down." Miss Mabel carefully slid the big flat pan off the cupboard and onto the table.

Janey sniffed three tea towels that covered the pan. "It smell sweet," she said.

"That's right," Jimmy agreed, not able to drag the suspense out further. He rolled a corner of a towel away.

"Cookies!" Harriet shouted, ready to grab while the others gawked.

"They look just like y'all," Jimmy snickered, looking at the brown cookie with big eyes made of baked-on, white icing. The big grinning mouth with missing teeth and skinny little arms and legs made everybody laugh until Jimmy said, "This one is you, Roberta."

Roberta stopped laughing. She heard the other laughter fade away.

"Company is first," Jimmy said with a smirk.

"Don't go out of your way to tease too hard now, Jimmy," Miss Mabel cautioned.

"No, ma'am," Jimmy replied, pulling all of the towels away.

"All of 'em look funny," Harriet said. That's what Jimmy had been doing—making cookies that looked like each of them, but in a silly sort of way, Roberta thought. Lena Mae's cookie had a long scar across the cheek. The mouth on Janey's cookie was frowning. Sadie's cookie looked like it was fast asleep, drooling from the mouth.

"Mine look like Humpty-Dumpty." Harriet bit into her cookie.

"Jimmy made some good cookies," Sadie praised.

"I'm gonna make mine last a long time," Lena Mae said, nibbling.

Roberta tried to do the same, but little bites made her mouth water for more. In a little while, the cookies had disappeared—Lena Mae's too.

Jimmy swaggered about with a pleased look on his face.

"How did you learn how to make cookies?" Roberta asked.

"Dewildera showed me a little bit," Jimmy admitted. "I made the icing by myself."

"I just showed him how to roll the dough," Dewildera said. "He read the recipe and did the rest."

Jimmy retrieved a wide-mouth jar top from the drawer. "Here's what I cut them out with. I rolled the arms and legs and stuck 'em on."

Roberta knew that it was time for her to thank Jimmy and to tell him how good his cookies tasted. She waited while Jimmy dropped the jar top back into the drawer.

"Thank you for making the ugliest, best cookies," Roberta gushed.

"Well, well," Miss Mabel said, chuckling. "Now I can give y'all your recitations for Children's Day at the schoolhouse. Got a recitation for you too, Roberta."

Roberta didn't join the instant chatter of voices that seemed to know the meaning of the big word Miss Mabel had used. "I'll get the book," Dewildera said as she ran upstairs.

"I'm big enough to have a lot to say this year," Janey bragged.

"I don't want a recitation; I'm gonna sing a solo," Jimmy said.

"Yeah, sing so low, nobody can hear you," Lena Mae teased.

Then Harriet yelled, "I hear the baby crying."

"Go to the well, Jimmy, and get his milk—his water bottle, too." Miss Mabel pushed herself away from the table. "'Bout time for him to wake up," she added with a smile.

Suppose a baby could go to sleep and never wake up, Roberta thought. Then everybody would stop talking about it.

"I got the baby, Mama," Dewildera called.

Roberta peeped out of the kitchen window. Jimmy was carefully pulling a clothesline out of the well. Two baby bottles were tied to the end of it. "Why did somebody put the bottles in the well?" she asked.

"Keep 'em cool," Lena Mae and her sisters answered at the same time.

"Our daddy said we gonna have ice in a box soon," Sadie added.

"Icebox," Lena Mae said quickly.

Roberta didn't care a thing about iceboxes. "Let's go outside and play," she said, nudging Lena Mae.

Too late. Suddenly, the kitchen buzzed with the presence of that whimpering baby. Out of the corner of her eye, Roberta saw Miss Mabel aim the bottle toward his face. That shut him up.

As soon as Dewildera opened the book she had brought downstairs, stuffed with loose pages, they heard the sound of Grampa's truck. Roberta tore out of the house and down the front steps.

"Wait, Roberta!" Lena Mae called. "Here's your recitation!"

"Gramma is here!" Roberta ran on to the truck. She looked back to see her friend waving a paper, midway across the yard.

"Did you thank Miss Mabel, and say bye to them all?" Gramma asked.

Just then, Miss Mabel appeared in the doorway without

the baby. "We enjoyed your lil' lady, Miss Louise." Lena Mae's mother spoke like she meant it.

Roberta fidgeted and glanced at the box of groceries in the back of the truck.

"Shore do appreciate it," Gramma said with a wave, not moving to make room in the truck for her grandchild.

Roberta turned back and ran past Lena Mae. "Thank you for dinner," she said to Miss Mabel, almost curtseying. Miss Mabel nodded and smiled. Roberta squeezed by and rushed inside as far as the stairway, yelling into the hubbub of voices, "Bye, everybody, thank you for the cookie, Jimmy." Not waiting to hear their reply, she ran back to Lena Mae.

"What ail you?" her friend asked, offering her the sheet of paper.

"Nothing." Roberta tried to smile, snatching the paper. "Thank you, Lena Mae—Gramma's waiting."

"Did you tell Miss Mabel and them you had a good time, child?" Grampa asked as the old truck pulled onto the road.

"Miss Mabel gave me this recitation for Children's Day," Roberta said instead of answering Grampa's question.

"That's your speech, child!" Gramma was excited. "You got to learn it."

"I know." Roberta didn't let on that she had just learned that *recitation* meant a speech of some kind. She folded the paper in half. Gramma didn't talk anymore. The truck was moving faster. That was good too. Soon she would be in her room—on her bed. She pushed a thought—that the baby in Mama's stomach might fall asleep and never wake up—out of her mind. Roberta took a deep breath. "It can't fall asleep until it comes out," she reasoned to herself.

"Whatchu thinking 'bout?" Gramma asked.

"Nothing!"

"Whatchu thinkin' 'bout when you ain't thinkin' 'bout nothing?"

"Something," Roberta let slip. "I mean nothing."

Grampa laughed at the joke as he backed the truck up to the front porch for unloading the box of groceries.

chapter eight

The clock said ten minutes before one o'clock when Roberta laid her recitation on the bureau beside her mother's letter. A letter she didn't want to answer. Roberta wondered how that baby was going to come out of her mother's stomach—"in almost three weeks" the letter had said. How? Like a cracking egg? No, Gramma and Daddy had looked funny when she mentioned that before. "I'll ask Gramma— she knows."

No matter how much she hung around her, Roberta couldn't think of how to put her question to Gramma. Then it got to be late evening, after supper. She sat on the porch with her grandparents and watched lightning bugs glow in the dusky air.

"Time for you to wash and go to bed, precious child," Gramma said softly.

I'll ask her tomorrow, Roberta thought, feeling tired. When Grampa's gone.

She washed her whole body because Gramma told her

to. "Been playing in dirt all day long." Gramma fussed about, throwing a towel on the bed and taking the tin tub away. Roberta soon piled into bed, her feet still wet.

The next day was Sunday and hotter than before—too hot to sit on the porch. Grampa didn't do anything except feed and water his mules and hogs, and feed the chickens. Roberta watched Gramma clean and boil a pullet to make sandwiches with what she called "store-bought" bread for dinner and supper. Still Roberta had not thought of how to put her question to Gramma.

A soft breeze blew down the hallway after they had eaten the last sandwiches with sliced tomatoes and cucumbers. Grampa put his fan down and tipped his chair against the wall.

"Where's your speech, child?" Gramma asked from her rocking chair. "Children's Day be here 'fore you know it. You can't be reading from the paper; you got to know it."

She raised herself from the cool linoleum floor and eased into her bedroom.

Gramma looked happy at the sight of the unfolded sheet of paper. "Read it out to me," Gramma said, not rocking. Grampa leaned forward.

Roberta stood tall and recited the piece for the first time:

Hurray, hurray! Some summer day
I'll get on a horse and gallop away

a-gallop, a-jallop
away on a spree
Over the bridge, down to the sea!
Hurray, hurray! Some summer day
I'll get on a ship and rollick away
a-rollick, a-frollick
a jolly good tune
Over the waves to Cameroon!
Hurrah, hurray! Some summer day
I'll get on a plane and zoom up high
a-soaring, a-roaring
way up in the clear
Over the clouds and back to here!

"John Allen would like this poem," she said when she'd finished. "He likes airplanes." Roberta didn't know where Cameroon was. She didn't understand the word *spree* either, but it sounded like a good time.

"You read good, child," Gramma said as she reached for the paper.

"That's a lot to have to learn," Grampa said, rubbing his chin.

That night, long after she had memorized the poem and laid it next to her wish-book dresses, Roberta stretched out on her bed and stared into the darkness of her room. If only she could have come right out and asked, "How will the baby

come out of Mama's stomach?" Maybe wishing the baby would fall asleep by itself and never wake up was more important. Yes, she would wish. Can't tell nobody about that idea, she thought to herself, flopping over onto her stomach. Not even Lena Mae. Suddenly Roberta felt sorry for running out of Lena Mae's house that day. She put it out of her mind and turned on her back and went to sleep.

All that week, one hot day ran into the other, sending Gramma and Grampa in search of a cool part of the house. They didn't talk much. Roberta guessed everybody in Scotland Neck was "shade hunting," as Grampa called it. Gramma cooked early in the morning to keep the heat down in the kitchen. There was nothing else to do.

Roberta put off answering her mother's letter again and again. She wondered about her skates, but she did not see John Allen Superman or Bay Often Ridin' Hay.

"Can't be movin' round in this scorching heat," Gramma snapped when Roberta started out to see if the boys were in Miss Ginny's yard.

"This July's been the worst for weather. Paper say almost one hundred degrees heat out there," Grampa added, his newspaper folded across his lap. "You been learning your speech?" He was grumpy too.

Roberta whirled around and said her poem from memory, running some of the words together.

"You got to put some feeling in it," Grampa suggested,

although both her grandparents looked satisfied with her recitation.

"I don't have to say it with expression now," Roberta said. "Gramma, how will the baby come out of Mama's stomach?" What made her ask right then? She did not know, but the question was out. Roberta felt beads of sweat running down the side of her face as she looked from one to the other.

Grampa cleared his throat, eased out of his seat, and walked down the back steps into the scorching sun.

"Why you ask such a grown-folks question?" Gramma asked.

"Because I want to know," Roberta said as simply as she could, sweating even more.

"The baby will come out when your mama give birth— when it's time for the baby to be born."

"But *where* will it come out from—"

"Think on what I just told you for a while." Gramma's firm voice filled the hallway.

"Yes, ma'am," Roberta said, taking short breaths. It was then that she got the idea to ask her mama.

"It's gonna cool off some, later on," Gramma said. "Go get my sewing box. Let me show you what I been working on."

"I want to write to Mama."

"That's good! You go write your mama—say something to your daddy too."

"Yes, ma'am." Roberta felt Gramma's eyes following her into the front room. The sticky stamps lay half curled on the table. Roberta pulled an envelope and three sheets of paper from the drawer and wrote.

Dear Mama,

I am fine. I hope you and Daddy are fine too.
I love you. I love Daddy.

Please write me back soon. Tell me how the baby
will come out of your stumick. I want to no soon.
I lerned a poem for the Childrens Day at the school.
It is a long poem. The sun is hot down hear. Lena
Mae will say a poem too.

I love you. I love Daddy. Write me back soon.

Your only child,
Roberta

"Mama will tell me," Roberta said to herself as she addressed the envelope. "She knows I love her and Daddy too." Pleased, she returned two sheets of unused paper to the drawer.

"Grampa, may I use one of your stamps?" Roberta yelled from the table.

"Yes, child," Grampa answered. "Come on 'way from that window—quick storm comin' up." He slammed the front door. "Supper got to wait."

Just then, a low rumbling and strong wind hit the house at the same time. Alarmed, Roberta ran into the hallway in time to see Gramma climbing up the back steps, out of breath. Zigzag lightning marked the sky, which was as black as soot.

"Had to make that ol' hen take her biddies in the coop," Gramma complained, closing the door. "She ain't got one lick of sense." Gramma eased into the rocker.

Streaks of lightning sent bursts of light from the open bedroom doors into the darkened hallway. Swirling wind sprayed the house with sand.

"I didn't know a storm was coming. I don't like storms." Roberta crept to Gramma's rocker and sat on the floor.

"Bound to happen, been so hot." Grampa's voice mixed with thunder that roared like a hundred wild animals. Rain poured. He tilted his ear toward the ceiling. "So glad it ain't hailing."

As soon as Roberta thought the lightning was gone for good, another loud clap of thunder made the house shudder.

"Have mercy," Gramma begged.

"Sound like the cloud 'bout ready to blow over," Grampa said.

Roberta crawled away from Gramma's rocker and rested herself against Grampa's straight-back chair.

Just like Grampa said, the storm blew over. Roberta

opened the door. Sunbeams sent bands of light from behind the low clouds. It was so quiet now and cool.

"We needed this rain," Grampa said, walking onto the porch. "All the peanuts, cotton, and corn and stuff just laughin' and grinnin'."

Roberta laughed. "Plants do not laugh."

"They do so," Grampa argued playfully.

"How can you tell?" Roberta asked, still smiling.

"See how them peanuts sparklin' with water on 'em? That's how they laugh and grin."

"Oh, Dave," Gramma cut in. "Y'all get ready to eat."

That night, before going to bed, Roberta stuck the stamp on her mother's letter.

The alarm clock roused everybody out of good sleeping weather the next morning. It was Saturday, the day when most country people went uptown. Roberta wanted to go this time. Before breakfast she took her letter to the mailbox. On the way back, she and John Allen spotted each other as he was carrying a bucket of water from the well.

"Where are my skates?" Roberta yelled.

"I been aimin' to tell you 'bout your skates." John Allen paused to switch the bucket from one hand to the other.

"Need the water, John Allen," Miss Ginny called from the back window, making her nephew rush inside.

"I'll just have to ask him again," Roberta said as she watched him go.

During breakfast, Gramma and Grampa chatted back and forth like they were happy again now that the sun was not so hot. Roberta joined in. "Gramma, if you and Grampa go uptown, can I go?"

"I reckon so," Grampa answered for his wife. "Got anything in mind to buy?"

"No, sir, I just want to see." Roberta smiled, excited. "I'm going to wear my pink dress."

"Fine by me," Gramma said. "Save the yellow one for Children's Day."

"I brought hair ribbons to match," Roberta remembered. "I need to wipe off my Sunday shoes."

By ten o'clock, they were ready. Gramma spread a towel over the middle of the seat. So I won't get my dress dirty, Roberta figured. Gramma's dark blue polka-dot dress looked new too. Grampa dressed in brown pants with suspenders cutting across his tan shirt.

The town of Scotland Neck was about three miles away. Grampa parked in the middle of the street with all the other cars and trucks. People strolled down the sidewalks, passing the grocery store and all the other shops.

It took a long time to weave through the crowd of people because everybody knew Gramma and Grampa. They introduced her. "This here's our little granddaughter— Want you to meet my lil' grand—Ain't seen you since my granddaughter came down here from Washington, D.C.—

This here's Robert's daughter." Some of them grabbed her hand and shook it. Some pushed their own children or grandchildren forward to meet her.

Roberta found herself saying "Howdy" or "Hi do" right back. It felt good to meet people who knew her father.

"Gettin' on time for us to tend our business," Grampa said as he tapped Gramma on the shoulder.

Roberta was not ready to move on but Gramma said "Yes, indeedy," so they pulled away. "While I make grocery, Dave, you go pay insurance and see 'bout your suit."

"Grampa, can I go with you?" Roberta put in quickly.

"I reckon so."

Roberta and Grampa strolled down the street. Shiny watches and necklaces caught sunlight in the window of Ray's Jewelry. High-heeled shoes reminded Roberta of her mother. The dress shop was next.

"Want a hot dog?" Grampa asked, slowing his step in front of Frozen Delight.

"Yes!" Roberta said, feeling hungry. "Can I have pop too?"

"Follow me," Grampa said as they entered the shop, filled with the smell of ice cream and hot dogs. Customers sprawled on three long church-like benches, eating hot dogs, drinking pop, and dipping out of ice cream cups. A huge ceiling fan whirled overhead.

"What'll it be, Dave?" a long-nosed man in a white apron asked politely from behind the counter.

"Two bottles of grape pop. Two hot dogs, fully dressed."
Roberta giggled.

"That mean we want 'em full of mustard, onions, chili,
relish—everything," Grampa explained, smiling down at her.

"Fully dressed," Roberta repeated. "People in Washington just name one by one all the things they want on their
hot dog."

"Yeah, and they waste a whole lot of time when they
could be eatin'." Grampa handed her a hot dog and a bottle
of pop.

Roberta sat beside Grampa on one of the benches. The
hot dogs and pop were finished off in no time. Grampa
gave her twenty cents for two cups of black walnut ice
cream—the best Roberta had ever tasted.

They had to stand in line to pay insurance. People didn't
talk except to answer a man who sat behind a caged window in the small room. There was nothing else to see, not
even a ceiling fan. At last, Grampa stood at the window.
After he pushed some money through an opening, they
were on their way to see about Grampa's suit.

"One more installment left," a woman with yellow hair
said as she took Grampa's five dollar bill and handed him a
piece of paper she had written on.

Gramma was standing on the street, holding a paper bag,
when the truck stopped in front of the grocery store.

Grampa left the motor running and went inside to get the groceries.

"I got barbecue from Ben's," she said as Roberta made room.

"We already had hot dogs, ice cream, pop," Roberta said.

"That's good," Gramma said, balancing the oily bag on her lap. "We'll have this for supper."

Grampa loaded the groceries and eased behind the steering wheel.

"I wish we could stay longer," Roberta remarked as they headed out of town. "Can we go back next Saturday?"

"They gonna have Children's Day practice at the schoolhouse next Saturday," Gramma informed her. "I promised Mabel I'd help her out."

"What day is Daddy coming for me?" she asked.

"When the baby's born," Grampa answered.

Roberta felt sad thinking about the baby and going back to Washington. She leaned her head on Gramma's shoulder.

The next day was Sunday. "A fine day for playing outdoors," Gramma said cheerfully a few times.

Roberta ignored the hint. She preferred being alone with Gramma and Grampa just then to playing with other children. She dug her crayons out of the suitcase. All day, pictures of horses, fairies, teddy bears, and flowers spread onto the hallway floor. She colored pictures, wallowed on her bed, and colored pictures and wallowed on her bed.

Before sundown, a knock sounded at the door.

John Allen, Bay, and Jimmy were on the porch. "We brought something back to Roberta," John Allen said to Grampa.

Grampa moved aside as Roberta approached the doorway.

"You nailed my skate wheels to pop boxes!" she said accusingly.

"I know it," John Allen explained. "It took a good lil' while for me to pry 'em loose. I aimed to come tell you 'bout that. Jimmy helped me bore the holes in the pop crates—show her how they work, Jimmy."

"You gonna like 'em," Jimmy said as he stuck his foot into the empty crate and pushed off. The skate wheels moved slowly.

"They'll do better at the end of the big road," John Allen bragged.

The boys had taken out the section that held the bottles in place. "They do roll some," Roberta agreed, eyeing the discolored crates that were about three feet high. "Tell you what," John Allen's eyes lit up. "How 'bout lettin' us put some paint on 'em."

"All right." Since they seemed more interested in the skates than she was at the moment, Roberta sent them away.

"I don't want to go back to Washington," Roberta suddenly blurted out when the boys had gone.

"What you say?" Grampa was surprised. Gramma held her jaw.

"I want to stay down here."

Grampa picked up a brown crayon and drew two big circles, linked together on the back of one of her pictures. "Look, Roberta," he said softly as he drew three smiling faces within the first circle. "This is me—this is Gramma—this is your daddy."

"So?"

"Family circles go round and round. Now, here we go round again startin' with your daddy this time." Grampa drew a smiling face in the other circle. "And here's your mama, here is Roberta, and here's the new baby."

"I don't want no baby there! Babies don't like me!" Roberta yelled and ran off to her room.

"You just tenderhearted right now, child," Gramma said gently. She and Grampa had followed Roberta to her room.

"Babies don't like me," Roberta repeated, backing into a corner. "Mama and Daddy and Aunt Emma—all of them won't love me if the baby is there."

"Let's talk on it some more," Grampa said calmly.

"I don't want to talk about it. I want to stay down here."

"Tell you what," Grampa began.

"No!" Roberta cried.

Grampa wouldn't take no for an answer. He grabbed Roberta and sat her on the chair. "You got to slow down and listen to reason," he said firmly but kindly. "You ain't making no sense. What make you think your mama and daddy won't love you no more?"

"Because they'll just love the new baby," Roberta said, wiping away her tears.

"Your mama write that in her letter—your daddy tell you that?"

"No, Grampa, but they—but they—" She couldn't continue.

"Let her rest for the night," Gramma told Grampa.

"She ain't tired, Louise," Grampa disputed. "Me and Roberta got some talkin' to do."

"About what?" Roberta sniffled.

"The family circle can have a whole lot of circles," Grampa began. "One day you gonna become a part of a circle different from the one you in right now. That way, the circle go round and round for years and years. Folks in the family circle love each other like your daddy and mama love you."

"You and Gramma love me too, don't you, Grampa?" Roberta asked.

"Course we do," her gramma cut in.

"I'm tired," Roberta said.

chapter nine

The next day was "a good day for giveaway," as Gramma and Grampa had said at breakfast. So the three of them picked tomatoes, cucumbers, and butter beans to give away to Miss Ginny and another woman named Miss Bethel.

"Some folks too old to plant a garden," Gramma said.

Roberta found searching through butter bean vines that had been trained to grow around an overhead wire frame exhausting. After throwing several handfuls of beans into the half full basket she complained, "My back aches."

"Pick," Grampa responded. "You too young to have a backache."

"Got to get this stuff to Miss Ginny and Miss Bethel this morning," Gramma chimed in.

"Yes, ma'am," Roberta said. "Do you have to give them so much?"

"Louise, did you hear your stingy grandchild?" Grampa laughed.

"I'm not stingy, I'm tired." Roberta looked at the full baskets of cucumbers and tomatoes they had already picked.

"And you want to stay down here?" Gramma teased.

"Yes, Gramma," Roberta said sincerely. Gramma and Grampa exchanged looks.

Finally, before twelve o'clock, Grampa drove off with the vegetables on the truck. He returned with nothing but the newspaper from the mailbox.

At the dinner table Grampa said he had seen Mister Joe Baker selling beans and other stuff for Miss Mabel. "I reckon Lena Mae and them been workin' too," Grampa said.

Roberta didn't complain about the work the next day. Grampa took a basket of tomatoes and yellow squash to sell to a man at the grocery store. "For spendin' change," he said.

Saturday rolled around—Children's Day practice at the schoolhouse—but still no letter from Washington.

"Mama didn't write to me," Roberta told Gramma. They passed the church and entered the school yard.

"You ain't got nothin' to worry 'bout," Gramma assured, quickening her steps.

They entered the long box-like building, which looked like it could use a coat of paint. It had an outside door for each of its three large rooms. All of the windows were on the back side of the building. Gramma went straight up front to sit at a desk beside Miss Mabel, below a put-together stage.

An upright piano took the corner space behind them.

"Sit here, Roberta." Lena Mae pointed to a nearby empty seat alongside her younger sisters. Dewildera and Harriet were not there, nor the baby. Jimmy, John Allen, and Bay walked in, making up the fifteen or so nervous-looking children. They sat quietly behind movable desks. Roberta didn't know most of the children.

"Time to start," Miss Mabel announced.

"What is she going to do?" Roberta whispered to Lena Mae.

"Call names, then we go up there and say our speeches," Lena Mae whispered back.

"Recitation, Bennett Leroy McDaniels," Miss Mabel announced. Leroy ran up on the stage and opened his mouth, but not a sound came out. Then Gramma prompted him and he remembered the words. "Next time, don't run, walk proud," Miss Mabel said to Leroy, who looked glad to be off the stage.

The list went on and on. One girl about the size of Roberta said the longest speech of all—with expression too, Roberta noticed. Right after, Miss Mabel called, "Recitation, Roberta Louise Robinson."

"I can say my speech," Roberta said to herself as she stood onstage. The first words, *Hurray, Hurray,* came out like a celebration. John Allen propped his elbows on the desk when he heard the last verse about airplanes. Then it was over. Gramma led the clapping at the end, reminding the boys to bow and the girls to curtsey.

"When will she call your name?" Roberta asked Lena Mae.

"I'm gonna sing with Jimmy," Lena Mae informed her proudly. "Mister Joe Baker had to work today, so we gonna practice at his house. He got a piano."

"Oh."

The next three speeches were a blur to Roberta. Sadie went last and had the shortest speech of all—just three lines. Everybody clapped loudly for the little girl.

Leaving the schoolhouse, the boys and girls separated to talk about "getting ready" for the great day. "My mama said she's taking me to the beauty parlor to get my hair done," an older girl told the others. "I'm wearing white shoes," another said. Yet another said, "My mama's making a new dress for me." No one in the group of girls knew what to say when Lena Mae told them, "We're not gonna get new stuff this year. My mama and daddy want to save money."

Roberta wished she had the courage to tell them about her new dresses or her new patent leather shoes. Ribbons matching her dress would make the only difference in her usual hairstyle, because braids were the only style Gramma knew how to do. So Roberta could look forward to wearing one braid hanging from the top of her head and two braids hanging down in the back.

Gramma and Miss Mabel saw to locking the schoolhouse door. Everybody wandered toward home. Roberta and Lena Mae listened to Gramma and Miss Mabel talk about the cakes and pies they were planning to make for the picnic that was to take place right after the program.

Up until Friday, the next week, there was still no letter from Washington. That day, nothing was more important than gathering cucumbers and cantaloupes for Grampa to sell uptown.

"Hush—you can hear 'em ripenin' on the vine." Grampa said something to make her laugh every time she was quiet for a while.

In all, they picked four big baskets of cucumbers and a half truck of cantaloupes before dinner.

"Can I go see how much money you get?" she asked as they loaded the truck.

"Yeah, climb in," Grampa said to Roberta's surprise, beckoning her.

"Is that John Allen runnin' this way?" Gramma said, shading her eyes.

"That's him," Grampa said. "Look like he waving something or other."

"Miss Louise!" John Allen was breathing hard by the time he reached the yard. "Aunt Ginny said the mailman put your letter from Washington, D.C., in her mailbox."

"Mama wrote to me!" Roberta exclaimed, grabbing at and missing the letter before John Allen pressed it into Gramma's hand.

"From Robert," Gramma's eyes skimmed the envelope as she ripped a single folded page away. She read,

> Dear Mama and Papa and Roberta,
>
> Helen had a boy last Sunday. He weighed nine pounds even. She is doing well and will come out of the hospital in two more days. We named the baby after you, Papa. How do you like that? Tell Roberta we can't wait until she sees her brother.
>
> Helen didn't want to name the baby after her daddy. She said you are the best, Papa.
>
> Kiss and hug Roberta for us. Tell her I'll drive down to get her early next Monday morning.
>
> Your son,
> Robert

"That's why she didn't answer my question," Roberta said. Gramma and Grampa stood silent.

"I gotta go and let Aunt Ginny know y'all didn't get no bad news," John Allen said, running out of the yard.

"Ain't we blessed, Louise?" Grampa said, at last. Tears

rolled down his face. "One grandchild named for you and one named for me—Dave Lewis Robinson."

"Oh, my gracious! Come here, Roberta. You got a little brother!" Gramma shouted. "Didn't I tell you your mama was gonna be all right?"

"Yes, ma'am," Roberta tried to answer without crying. Gramma's smothering kisses and hugs went on and on, but Roberta didn't mind. It kept her mind off the baby. The baby was the one making everybody happy.

"I have to pack my things," Roberta said at last.

"We'll get to that," Gramma said, eyeing Grampa.

"Well, I gotta get this truck of stuff uptown." Grampa closed the tailgate, unable to stop smiling. "I got me two grandchildren," he said to himself before driving out of the yard.

"Dave, you be careful," Gramma warned. "And don't forget your suit."

The truck disappeared into a cloud of road dust. Roberta wanted to be the only grandchild.

"Is nine pounds a lot, Gramma?" Roberta asked as they went to the kitchen.

"That's a lot of weight for a new baby," Gramma replied. "Here, take this bucket."

"You think Mama is glad about the baby?" Roberta said, following Gramma to the pump, swinging the bucket.

"She ought to be—your daddy too. They got two fine children now. Put the bucket under there and hold it still." Water splashed off the rim and down the front of Roberta's dress.

Gramma didn't fuss about her wet dress. Roberta wanted to talk about this baby that had come out of her mother's stomach in some unexplained way. For sure, he had taken Grampa's name and earned Grampa's smile. Could she still wish that her brother would fall asleep and never wake up? Yes, she answered her own question. I don't feel like a sister.

"I think babies are a lot of trouble, Gramma," Roberta said matter-of-factly when the bucket was full.

"We got a whole mess of things to get done before Children's Day," Gramma said firmly.

"I know," Roberta answered, opening the screen door for Gramma. "I'm not tired. I can help. I'm big enough to bring in the wood. I can dry the dishes too."

"That's good, child," Gramma replied.

Carrying the wood and drying the dishes was easy. She swept the hallway too.

Grampa honked the horn to let them know he had returned. His smile lasted throughout suppertime.

Saturday, the same smile was pasted on Grampa's face. At bedtime that night, Roberta heard Gramma ask, "Dave, did you tell anybody 'bout the baby?"

"Just a few folks," Grampa said proudly.

Roberta strained to hear Gramma say, "If you told a few, you told everybody."

"It ain't no secret," Grampa said.

I have a secret, Roberta thought to herself. I have a secret wish; I hope it comes true.

chapter ten

Children's Day began at six in the morning on Sunday, as Gramma's baking, frying, and boiling made the kitchen feel hot as an oven. The smell of apple pie and pound cake kept them hungry even after breakfast.

Gramma rushed them into cleaning away eggshells and washing mixing bowls. The turnips and greens had to be washed in the big tub at the pump.

"I didn't know you knew how to help cook," Roberta teased, pumping the water.

"Your Gramma puts me to work like this every year," Grampa complained.

"Well, you're still smiling," Roberta observed.

By one-thirty the roll-top trunk was so packed with food, it took Gramma and Grampa both to hoist it onto the truck bed. Then they were on their way.

Gramma wore a pink dress and a big floppy hat to match. Grampa's new suit was gray.

"Folks be gittin' here early this year," Grampa said as he parked the truck in the shade along with the other cars.

"Well, there's Good Soul," Gramma said of a little man with a mustache who was busy searching the yard.

"What's he going to do with those sticks and pieces of wire?" Roberta wanted to know.

"He think somebody might trip and get hurt," Grampa said. "So he picks up all kinds of junk. That's why they call him Good Soul."

"Oh." Families caught Roberta's eye. Everybody was starched and ironed and careful not to walk into the deep sand in their Sunday shoes. Toddlers were lifted to grassy areas. Dewildera carried the baby. Harriet and Sadie followed.

Lena Mae wore a flowered dress. Her hair was fixed in bangs. Jimmy found John Allen and Bay and Joe Bill, Mister Joe Baker's boy. The four of them walked about with serious looks.

The recitations were first on the program. The grown folks clapped long and loud for everybody. Roberta said her speech fine—and with feeling.

Jimmy and Lena Mae sang the best. Grown folks stood up to clap for them. Roberta could see the bald spot on the top of tall Mister Joe Baker's head when he bowed from the waist.

At last, the trunks and baskets were laid open under the trees. Food of every kind was spread out on long tables for people to pick and choose.

With Lena Mae at her elbow, Roberta didn't bother to talk to the other children. The two of them sampled deviled eggs from two baskets. Miss Ginny's barbecue smelled so good. Turnip greens and Gramma's fried chicken were Roberta's favorite.

"Roberta, you and Lena Mae save room for sweets," Gramma reminded the girls.

"Yes, ma'am," they said together and popped another deviled egg into their mouths.

They meandered to the opposite end of the tables, putting more chicken and ham on their plates.

"Let's go over here and sit down." Roberta spotted two empty chairs nearer to the churchyard. "People in the country have good times."

"I bet people in Washington do too," Lena Mae said. Then she mentioned cautiously, "We heard the news— your mama had a boy baby. You glad to be goin' back?"

"I don't know," Roberta said. "I want some of Gramma's cake before it's all gone."

"I'm already full." Lena Mae picked at the last piece of ham on her plate.

"Me too." Roberta changed her mind. Gramma's pound cake must be all gone by now, anyway, she thought.

"Lena Mae, you seen Jimmy and Janey?" Miss Mabel seemed uneasy as she shifted the baby in her arms.

"No, ma'am." Lena Mae scanned a bunch of children balancing their plates on the schoolhouse steps. Jimmy and Janey were not among them.

"I sent him to pull a cool milk bottle out 'n the well 'bout twenty minutes ago now."

"Janey went with him?"

"Yeah." Miss Mabel started toward the road.

"There's Dewildera." Roberta spotted the oldest sister in a group of her friends.

"There's Janey." Lena Mae pointed to her sister, who was running toward them.

"Jimmy fell in!" Janey hollered. "Mama! Jimmy fell in the well."

"What?!" Miss Mabel cried.

"That boy of Mabel's fell in the well!" Good Soul shouted to the grown people.

A whirlwind of scattering plates, running feet, and shouting voices emptied the school and churchyard as more than half the crowd took off on foot.

Lena Mae and her younger sisters crammed into somebody's car with Miss Mabel.

"You stay here, child," Gramma ordered, jumping into the truck with Grampa.

"I don't want to stay by myself!" Roberta yelled after the

trunk, which went popping down the road faster than she had ever seen it go.

"You can stay with me," Dewildera said.

Roberta jerked around, astonished to see Lena Mae's oldest sister sitting behind one of the tables, holding the baby. Harriet sat beside her. "You didn't go?"

"Mama wanted me to keep the baby and Harriet out'n the way."

Roberta didn't know what to say as she sat down. Dewildera was not crying. Harriet was not crying. The baby was bouncing up and down. "I'm scared about Jimmy," she said softly. Suppose Jimmy went to sleep and never woke up like in her secret wish? "Are you scared, Dewildera?"

"Mama told me not to worry. Here, hold Junior while I look down the road."

"He's going to cry," Roberta protested, knowing that if the baby cried, she would cry too.

"No he won't." Dewildera said, wrapping Roberta's arms around the baby. She trotted toward the road.

Roberta guessed that it was okay this time that she hadn't washed her hands.

"Mama told me not to worry too," Harriet said to herself.

Roberta felt baby drool on her arm, and it didn't bother her one bit.

Dewildera came back and sat down. "I'll take him back now," she said, reaching out her hands.

"Let me hold him?" Roberta asked as she brushed the side of her face on Junior's soft hair.

Dewildera nodded and looked off. Harriet sat in Dewildera's lap. Junior kept on gibbering and drooling.

Roberta was still holding Junior when the first car returned with Miss Mabel. Lena Mae spilled out of the backseat first; her dress was smeared with mud. Then Sadie and Janey jumped out. Their clothes were muddy too. Jimmy was the last one. Red mud caked his best clothes and shoes; even his face was muddy.

Harriet ran to her mother. Dewildera grabbed the baby. Roberta ran to Jimmy and threw her arms around his neck. "You didn't die!" she said, hoping no one would say anything about the tears running down her face. Then her best dress was stained with red mud too. Jimmy let everybody hug him. Roberta hugged Lena Mae and Miss Mabel too.

"If it hadn't been for Good Soul..." Mister Joe Baker shook his head. "Good Soul saved Jimmy's life."

Good Soul didn't come back to the schoolhouse. Roberta found out that Jimmy didn't want to soil his best pants so he'd climbed up on the wash bench to pull the baby bottle out of the well. That's when he lost his balance and grabbed one of the chains for drawing buckets of water. But he fell feet first about five feet before swinging to the top of the wood casing. There was so much slack in the chain, Jimmy couldn't hang long without falling to the bottom of the deep well. Good Soul got there just in time. He was small enough to be lowered down the well and pull Jimmy out.

Unruffled now, the grown folks collected children, empty plates, baskets, and trunks. The sun was sinking and it was time to go home.

"Good-bye!" Roberta hugged Lena Mae again, then Sadie. Janey said good-bye leaning against Dewildera. Harriet hung on to Miss Mabel's skirt. Someone had given Bay Often Ridin' Hay, John Allen Superman, and Miss Ginny a ride home.

"What a week," Grampa said on the way out of the school yard. "A new grandbaby, a new suit, good eats, and a new lease on life for Jimmy."

"Good gracious," Gramma replied. "Child, your daddy will be here early tomorrow morning."

"I know," Roberta said. "Gramma, Grampa, I'm sorry for what I did."

"What did you do?" Grampa asked, sounding confused.

"I wished—I didn't want—"

"Child, you ain't got to be sayin' nothin' 'bout nothin'" Gramma intoned.

"Something might be wrong, Louise," Grampa said. "Let her talk."

"Dave, I know everything's all right," Gramma insisted.

That night, Gramma and Grampa helped pack her suitcases. No one knew how early her father was going to arrive the next day.

"Knowing Robert, he'll start out right after midnight and get down here by seven o'clock in the morning," Grampa figured. It was nine o'clock that night when Roberta packed her clock. Gramma had washed and dried her yellow dress. Roberta went to sleep by the ticking sound coming from her suitcase.

The forgotten alarm and Gramma sounded at the same time. "He's pulling in here," Gramma shouted.

Roberta leaped out of bed and ran off the porch to jump into her daddy's arms. In a little while she asked, "How is Mama? Is the baby all right?"

"Of course, baby girl." Her daddy patted her on the head as they stepped onto the porch.

"What's going on in this sleepy house?" he joked.

"Packin' up, gettin' ready to go!" Gramma laughed as if she was singing.

"Is Mama still in the hospital? Does Mama have to stay in bed? What time are we leaving?" Roberta asked excitedly.

"Slow down, child," Grampa said. "I had to cut your alarm off," he said, smiling out.

"How've you been, Papa?" her daddy said, not answering her questions.

"Pretty good, pretty good." They shook hands and went into the front room.

Roberta rushed to bathe and get dressed while Gramma was making breakfast. The grown-up voices filled the house.

"Dave Lewis a healthy little fellow," her daddy reported. "The doctor said Helen is doing real good."

"We so glad, son." Roberta could imagine Grampa smiling and nodding his head in agreement with Gramma.

"I do so thank y'all for helping me out," her daddy said.

"You know you ain't got to thank us for that," Grampa replied.

Roberta unbraided her hair and brushed it back. "This is the way I'm going to wear my hair today," she thought, looking into the mirror a long time.

"Be quiet," Gramma directed in a whisper when Roberta stepped into the hallway. "Your daddy in the front room sleeping."

Roberta followed her grandmother into the kitchen, where they ate in silence. Now she was going home, to *her* home.

Around nine-thirty, her daddy startled her by yawning loudly. He sat down at the kitchen table.

"Good sleep," he said, watching Gramma fix his plate. "Strong coffee, Mama," he requested.

The car was loaded by ten o'clock. "Y'all just get on in that car and get on the road," Grampa instructed. "Or nightfall will catch you. Write us soon as you git there."

"All right, Papa," her daddy said, shaking his father's hand and hugging his mama.

"Thank you, Gramma. Thank you, Grampa."

"We enjoyed you so much, child." Gramma hugged Roberta and led her to the car.

"Shore did," Grampa said, opening the back door.

"Bye Gramma, bye Grampa."

Then the car was backing away from the chinaberry tree. Her daddy drove onto the dirt road. The top of Lena Mae's house stood out at the bottom of the road. They passed Miss Ginny's house. John Allen, Bay, and Jimmy were waving for her daddy to stop the car at the big pine tree.

"They have my skates!" Roberta rolled down the window.

"We got Roberta's skates ready." John Allen had painted one of the crates to look like the nose of an airplane. Airplane wings stuck out from the side of the crate. The other crate resembled a big truck of some kind.

"Y'all can have them," Roberta said. "Bye, John Allen Superman. Bye, Jimmy. Bye, Bay Often Ridin' Hay." John Allen's going to fly airplanes some day, she thought.

The car pulled onto the paved road. Her daddy was smiling.

"Daddy," Roberta asked before they reached Emporia. "Tell me about Dave Lewis."

"Oh, he's something else. You know he grinned in his sleep the other night?"

"Can I hold him?"

"Yes, indeed. You're the big sister."

"Know what, Daddy?" Roberta asked after a while.

"What?"

"I'm in the family circle with you and Mama and Dave Lewis, and the circle goes round and round."

"I know that."

"I do too, now."

"That's good, baby girl."

Roberta smiled. "I wonder how you make your backbone slip," she said to herself.

"What?"

"Nothing."

The car sped in the direction of Washington, D.C., back to her mama and to Dave Lewis.

ALICE McGILL is an award-winning author and professional storyteller. She has toured to collect and tell stories in thirty-nine states, Canada, the West Indies, and South Africa. She lives with her husband in Columbia, Maryland.

ALSO BY ALICE McGILL

MOLLY BANNAKY
illustrated by Chris Soentpiet

An ALA Notable Book
Winner of the 2000 Jane Addams Picture Book Award
Winner of the 2000 IRA Childrens Book Award

★"The oversized format and stunning watercolor paintings turn this fictionalized biography of the grandmother of Benjamin Banneker into an exciting visual experience."
—*School Library Journal,* starred review

MILES' SONG
A Bank Street College of Education Best Book of the Year

"The novel reads like a suspense thriller."—*The Bulletin*

"An enlightening and absorbing story about a truly memorable character."—*School Library Journal*

IN THE HOLLOW OF YOUR HAND: SLAVE LULLABIES
pictures by Michael Cummings

★"A memorable aural and visual journey into the past."
—*Publishers Weekly*, starred review

"Part of the oral tradition, this moving collection of thirteen folk lullabies is a powerful way to communicate what family life was like under slavery."—*Booklist*

"A book that will become a keepsake in many homes, including mine."—*New York Times Book Review*

SHANE EVANS, a fine artist, has illustrated many acclaimed books for children including *Osceola: Memories of a Share-cropper's Daughter*, which won a Boston Globe–Horn Book Honor Book award and the Orbis Pictus Award for Outstanding Nonfiction for Children. He lives in Kansas City, Missouri.